Watching her with lustrous brown eyes, he motioned her to sit, which she found herself doing. "What are you doing here, Miss Caldicott? What is your business at Savaron Hall?"

"I came on the stage from London just as Lady Linville suggested in her letter."

"What letter?" asked Hugh.

"The one to Mrs. Mellow, my employer. She asked me to come as her companion, and it sounded—"

"I would like to see that letter," he interrupted.

"Well, you cannot. It's gone with Mrs. Mellow to York. You can write to her but very likely you won't believe her any more than you believe me!" Clio's voice quivered with indignation. "There certainly was a letter."

Showing that he was not unreasonable, Hugh said, "All right. So there was. I would like to see who wrote it."

"Who wrote it! It was signed 'Mary Linville.' Couldn't she have done so?"

"Unless someone else signed her name." He pursed his lips as if determined not to believe her.

"Why would anyone do that? Good gracious! There is nothing mysterious about hiring a companion." Truly, he was as impossible as he was handsome.

"I wonder if she was afraid and wanted you to protect her."

"And how much protection would I be? Ridiculous," said Clio.

"You could have tried batting those pretty gray eyes at any assailant to distract him."

Indignant at such obvious nonsense in a serious matter, Clio quite ignored his attention to her eyes.

"Good day, Miss Caldicott." He strode off, both he and she wondering if he could suspect her of a crime.

"Blast that man," she muttered to herself. . . .

A LADY DECIDES

Dorothea Donley

Zebra Books
Kensington Publishing Corp.
http://www.zebrabooks.com

ZEBRA BOOKS are published by

Kensington Publishing Corp.
850 Third Avenue
New York, NY 10022

Zebra and the Z logo Reg. U.S. Pat. & TM Off.

First Printing: October, 1999
10 9 8 7 6 5 4 3 2 1

Printed in the United States of America

One

"How very odd," said Mrs. Mellow. The pile of letters on her plump knees slid to the floor as she examined one both through and above her spectacles.

Clio, who was kneeling on the floor to add a last dress to Mrs. Mellow's modest trunk, sat back upon her heels and asked encouragingly, "Odd?"

"Well, my dear—I really don't know—" Mrs. Mellow rattled the paper. "Listen to this: 'Dear Mrs. Mellow, Henry tells me that you are soon off to visit your son, so your delightful companion, Miss Caldicott, will be at loose ends. Would she, perhaps, be willing to come to me for a time? I am in need of a companion myself. If this is agreeable to her, send her along on Friday to the inn at Scudderfield and I will have a carriage meet her. The morning stage to Bath is due here about five. Mary Linville.' "

It was true that Mrs. Mellow was keeping her flat while visiting York, and Clio would be able to await her return in lonely comfort. Nevertheless, Clio felt that her "ends" could not be looser. She exclaimed, "How kind!"

"So it may sound, child, but I do not know anyone named Mary Linville." Mrs. Mellow threw down the bothersome letter. Although her blue eyes wore a perpetual expression of astonishment because life was unexpected, now they looked indignant. "Why are you packing for me? Surely that is Agnes's duty!"

"Agnes is giving your traveling dress a final pressing while the water heats for your bath," Clio replied. "If Agnes can do two things at once, surely I can do the third."

"You are teasing me," Mrs. Mellow accused. She was beginning to struggle from the confines of her chair.

Clio sprang to help her mistress.

For nearly two years the ladies had enjoyed a pleasant relationship, all due to Mr. Lambton at St. Giles. When Mrs. Mellow's son, Francis, married a wealthy mill owner's daughter and went to live in York, Mrs. Mellow was left quite alone. Mr. Lambton had the happy thought of introducing her to Miss Caldicott, a faithful at St. Giles, who had lost her only parent and needed a home.

How Francis Mellow had succeeded in attaching a rich wife Clio did not know. She had seen him only twice, briefly, and had no opinion of his assets. Perhaps the wife of Francis liked his chill good looks. Or perhaps she liked his genteel tailoring.

As they moved toward Mrs. Mellow's bedchamber, the round little lady twinkled up at Clio, saying, "To think I will travel so far north!" And Clio, having her own thoughts, answered, "I think Mrs. Francis Mellow must be a charming person."

"Do you? Why do you say so?"

"Because," explained Clio, "she wrote you such a gracious invitation."

Mrs. Mellow looked at her, eyebrows raised. "But, my dear, of *course* Francis told her what to say!"

Francis, thought Clio, could jolly well have written his mother himself. Never wanting to cause her mistress grief, she returned bracingly, "You will have a splendid time."

She guided Mrs. Mellow around the trunk and various other disrupted furnishings. "I will take you to your room and then go down to see if Agnes is ready

with the water." Mrs. Mellow being in no way infirm
but enjoying attention, they progressed slowly.

They found a tub and cold water waiting behind a
screen. All that was needed was Agnes with the hot
bucket. Clio left Mrs. Mellow at her dressing stool
while she descended to the kitchens.

The house was one of a row of town houses in a
street off Soho Square with several pleasant rooms on
the first floor which Mrs. Mellow occupied. Her son's
departure had emptied a room for Clio. It was a sunny
room with a sideways view of the square and yellow
walls and hangings which exactly suited her temperament. The landlady and her boy shared the second
floor with a physician's apprentice, while Agnes and
other servants slept under the low ceiling of the third
floor. The kitchens were open to all. Assorted squab-
bles entertained the Lesser Orders, and the lowest
level was consequently the jolliest.

There Clio found Agnes just setting aside her iron.
A tweeny was filling a bucket from the fire.

"Let me take the dress, Agnes," Clio said, "while
you bring the bucket. Are your clothes packed?"

"Yes, miss, but I wisht it was you going," Agnes
grumbled. "I rode a stage once and my stomach don't
forget it. Might as well hang me by my knees from an
axle."

Chuckling, Clio replied that Mrs. Mellow could not
manage without her Agnes. "Besides," she added,
"you will be riding as far as Grantham with Dr. Dudley
in his own coach, and I am sure he has the best and
most comfortable of everything."

This confidence in the good doctor's coach was
based solely on the knowledge that he was the late Mr.
Mellow's devoted friend and Mrs. Mellow's physician.
As Agnes knew him also to be the dispenser of a coin
now and then, she ceased to carp, though her frown
did not slacken.

Clio led the way upstairs. "You will be seeing wonderful sights of England," she said.

Agnes complained that she would not see much. "All sliding away from me, miss!"

Clio halted on one step and looked back. "Oh, Agnes, does it make you queasy to ride backward? Then you must ask Dr. Dudley to change places with you."

"Me? Oh, miss, I'd never," Agnes cried, scandalized.

"Nonsense. Dr. Dudley is a medical doctor. He likes to make people *well.*"

After they had gone in to Mrs. Mellow, Agnes to deliver the hot bucket, and Clio to hang the dress, Clio left Mrs. Mellow to the services of her maid, while she removed to Mrs. Mellow's drawing room to prepare it for Dr. Dudley's coming. She scooped up the letters that her mistress had cast aside, mostly unread, and tossed them into the trunk, added a shawl, and fastened the lid. So much for that. It remained only to shove a chair or two into place and plump up cushions. Dr. Dudley would not notice much, anyway.

Clio sighed as she scanned the room. It was a pleasing blend of dark woodwork and wainscot with white walls and fabrics in shades of pink. She did not know if the choice of colors was Mrs. Mellow's or the landlady's. Certainly, the furniture belonged to Mrs. Mellow, being substantial, comfortable, not lavish in design or quantity but refined. No reptile feet!

She was fortunate to have found a home here.

And she would miss the old lady who was so indulgent, calling her "dear child," treating her like a daughter, not stinting on meals or candles, letting her wear her hair caught back with a ribbon with tendrils of gold curling about her face instead of being twisted into a severe knot. Mrs. Mellow preferred, she said, to look at youthful bloom—no repressed spinster for *her*—no, indeed!

Papa had never been able to afford fancy clothes for Clio, just a few simple pastel frocks suitable to her age. Not even a black one for mourning, but dear Mrs. Mellow said it would be a shame to smother Clio's sunny disposition in mourning clothes.

"I cannot abide crows!" declared Mrs. Mellow, giving her pink, green and blue hair-ribbons to wear.

At seventeen, when she came to live there, Clio was both old and young. Her mind was lively, yet her manner was oddly adult from having lived quietly with her studious father and knowing only his scholarly friends. Of worldly matters, she knew nothing. By age nineteen she had readily embraced Mrs. Mellow's amiable views of everything.

Everything except, of course, the supposed superiority of Mr. Francis Mellow. How Mrs. Mellow had raised such a stuffed shirt she could not fathom.

The door to Mrs. Mellow's bedchamber opened, and although Clio could hear voices, she could distinguish no words. Presently, Agnes emerged with buckets.

"All finished," she said. "You're wanted, miss."

"Here is our key, Clio, my dear," said Mrs. Mellow when the girl entered. "I wish Francis had said I could bring you, too. What will you do while I am gone?"

"Do not worry, ma'am! I can be easy here, although of course I shall miss you. I thought—perhaps—well, I might venture to Brighton for a few days. You never let me spend my salary—so generous you are to me—and I have enough saved for a little jaunt. It would be exciting to see the sea." Clio set Mrs. Mellow's bonnet on her head and held a mirror for her to see her reflection.

"To be sure you deserve a vacation," Mrs. Mellow asserted.

"I do not feel I need one," Clio answered. "You must not fret about me. *My* only concern is that you may not return. I would be sorry for myself in that case, but it would be fine for you if you could settle happily with your relatives in York."

"Not likely," said Mrs. Mellow tersely.

"At any rate, we will exchange letters, won't we?" Clio asked, adjusting the bow of the bonnet and standing back to admire the effect.

"Certainly we will," agreed her mistress. "Do I hear a carriage?"

They went into Mrs. Mellow's drawing room just in time to receive Dr. Dudley.

"Well, well, you are prompt," he said, beaming cheerfully at Mrs. Mellow from under craggy brows. He was a large man with a mien that inspired confidence. As always, he appeared in well-tailored gray and the whitest of cravats. Even his hands were exquisitely white. So reassuringly sanitary.

"Only because you were kind enough, Harry, to make a later start than I dare say you would have liked," she replied. "And here is Agnes with her valise."

"Good, good." He motioned to the two grooms who had accompanied him into the room, and they went off with the baggage.

There was a small flurry of admonitions. Clio handed Mrs. Mellow her reticule, Dr. Dudley said farewell, and Mrs. Mellow kissed Clio warmly.

"Remember. Write, dear," reminded Mrs. Mellow.

Clio followed the threesome into the hall and stood at the outer door, watching them go down the flight to the street. She heard Dr. Dudley say, "Fine gel."

To which Mrs. Mellow responded, "Yes, yes. I worry about her, Harry. She does not realize how pretty she is. . . ."

Clio gently closed the door and, lips twitching, turned to examine herself in the hall mirror.

Was she pretty?

She really was not sure, for she knew so few young ladies with whom to compare herself. Not many fashionable young women attended St. Giles Church or her papa's seminars.

The smile lingered in her eyes. *They* were large enough, gray with thick lashes. Her mouth was neat, neither exceptionally full nor exceptionally small, and her delicate nose straight. Perhaps her sunny blond hair was her best feature, but she had no way of knowing if blondes or brunettes were fashionable.

Once, when she and Mrs. Mellow were enjoying refreshments at a tearoom, a lady and natty gentleman entered. Except for noticing the man's petulant expression, Clio scarcely observed him for her eyes were fastened upon the gorgeous lady. Flashing black eyes, a wing of black hair under a lilac bonnet with lilac plumes, and an alluring smile of crimson lips!

"Oh, Mrs. Mellow, how beautiful," she had whispered. "Look to your left."

Mrs. Mellow had looked.

"Haymarket ware," she had answered with a decided sniff.

Clio had not exactly understood the meaning of "haymarket ware," but she had recognized her employer's disapproval.

Splendid. Exotic. But not a lady. And therefore not to be considered an example of true beauty.

She sighed now and shook her head at the girl in the mirror. Then she returned to the empty apartment. There were faint sounds of hooves from the square, but inside all was silent.

For a time Clio busied herself by remaking Mrs. Mellow's bed with fresh sheets and storing away the few things that Agnes, in her haste, had not been able to tend to properly. Her own room was always tidy.

Still, the morning was not half done.

She felt very lonely.

"I daresay Mr. and Mrs. Lambton will come to call—and some of Papa's friends, but maybe not today . . .

and maybe not this week," she told herself, feeling even more lonely as she mentally enumerated the possibilities.

She would like to walk to the nearest shops and spend some time without spending money, yet even in her most modest frock and drabbest shawl she might be exposed to unwelcome advances. Had she escorted Mrs. Mellow or had Mrs. Mellow chaperoned her? Going about alone was sure to be hazardous, which was not something she had thought about when Mrs. Mellow planned her own trip to York.

"Well, I must not stay here and mope!" she said aloud. "I must go as I planned to Brighton. No one will notice me in the crowds there. Besides, my bonnet is very plain. Yes, and the old cloak that Mrs. Mellow left behind is wonderfully shabby, and I do not think she would mind my using it."

She started toward her own bedchamber thinking with a chuckle that if worse came to worst she might dust her hair to look gray. Only a few steps from Mrs. Mellow's doorway the sobering thought smote her: *I will be just as lonely in Brighton as London!*

A fresh, hot cup of tea presently revived her spirits, which were naturally optimistic and could not remain oppressed for long, so that her mind turned to Henry-with-no-last-name and the unknown Mary Linville who had asked her to come for an unspecified time. Well, why not? Whoever Henry was, he knew about *her* and Mrs. Linville sounded ladylike, not at all diabolical. She thought she remembered "Scudderfield" and something about stages.

It became imperative to find Mrs. Linville's letter, but of course it had vanished.

In a whirl of activity, Clio searched Mrs. Mellow's room and the drawing room without success. She knew it could not be lurking in her own room, so she went down to the kitchens (for no good reason) and eventually out to scratch in the dustbin.

Failure.

Thereupon, she seated herself on an overturned urn rested her chin upon her hand, and commanded herself fiercely to *think*.

In no time at all she retrieved two useful clues: Bath stage and Friday.

Good heavens! No time to answer Mrs. Linville's letter, and in any case, the lady seemed blithely to expect her. But *Friday* was *tomorrow*.

"I haven't a booking," she moaned, as she caught up her skirts and charged up the staircase to the second floor to bang upon the landlady's door, calling, "Jed! Jed!"

There was no reply.

She rapped again. And a third time, at which point the door across the landing opened and the physician's apprentice came out, smoothing his shaggy blond hair hurriedly.

"Is something wrong, Miss Caldicott?" he asked, regarding her with an adoring expression which she took to be myopia.

"Oh, Mr. Thatch . . . I wanted Jed. I'm very anxious to take the Bath stage tomorrow morning and was hoping I could send the boy to book a seat for me—as far as Scudderfield."

Young Mr. Thatch, being too gentlemanly to ask the reason for her hurry, blushed and said, "No difficulty. I will be glad to go for you." If he wondered how long she would be away, he controlled himself and did not ask.

"But I must not impose," she exclaimed.

"No imposition at all," he replied happily. "Bath to Scudderfield. Friday morning. I will attend to it at once."

Before she could protest further, he ran lightly down the steps and let himself out the street door.

Astonished, Clio descended more slowly. She was accustomed to thinking of young men as dangerous, with the result that she had seldom exchanged more than a civil "how-do-you-do?" with poor Mr. Thatch. It was surprising to find him so willing to be of service to a lady who had not been much better than coolly civil.

Mr. Lambton would be sure to say something about angels all around us, she thought guiltily, as she began to pack her belongings.

In two years her clothes had become more stylish, due to the influence of Mrs. Mellow, who had lost interest in fashion for herself, preferring to smarten up the girl. It had been a gradual process so that Clio was scarcely aware of the change. While Mrs. Mellow accommodated her own girth with easy, flowing garments of best materials and workmanship, she coaxed Clio into tucks here and simple ruchings there. From time to time she gave her a gossamer scarf or lavender kid gloves, until both ladies were quite elegant, each in her own style.

Mr. Thatch must have galloped at least part of the way, for he returned just as Clio was laying the last frock into her trunk. When he knocked at Mrs. Mellow's drawing room door, Clio went hesitantly to answer. It would not be proper to let him *in* while she was unchaperoned, yet it seemed ungracious to speak through a half-opened door. She stepped into the hallway, prepared to leap back to safety if need be.

It was worry for nothing. Mr. Thatch, if threadbare and somewhat rumpled, had the instincts of a gentleman. He kept his distance, reporting: "All is arranged. A seat is promised to you."

"Oh, thank you, thank you!" cried Clio, her gratitude spilling over because of her guilt at suspecting his motives.

"But," he added, "the coach leaves at seven sharp which means you will have to leave home no later than six and I will not—cannot—let you go alone to the posting house at that hour. You will let me escort you, will you not?"

He was quite firm, though somewhat red with embarrassment.

She agreed, thanked him, and said, "You are very kind."

Two

When Mr. Thatch knocked gently at exactly six the next morning, Clio was ready and waiting, for she had slept fitfully all night and was out of bed and dressing by five.

"You are right on time!" she greeted him.

"Yes, thank goodness," he replied. "I was afraid I would oversleep."

"So was I."

They smiled timidly at each other and relaxed in manner, both having abandoned false speculations. With Mr. Thatch carrying Clio's small trunk jauntily on his shoulder, they walked to the street corner near the square, where they found a cabbie napping in his hackney and his horse drowsing on three legs.

Young man, young lady, and trunk were soon on their way through silent streets that echoed with the clop of horse hooves. As they neared the posting house more people were visible at their occupations—shutters opening, news vendors taking station at corners, crossing sweepers cleaning for first walkers.

"I must insist on one thing," Mr. Thatch said boldly when Clio began to fumble with her reticule. "I will pay our driver."

"It would not be right!" she protested.

But Mr. Thatch, whom she assumed to be chronically short of funds, insisted she must consider his self-respect, and Clio, who valued her own self-respect, acquiesced.

At the posting house all was turmoil as several coaches prepared for runs in various directions. Clio was thankful to have Mr. Thatch to find her vehicle, stow her trunk, see that she paid the right fare to the right person, and settle her in a forward-facing seat— not a window seat, unfortunately, but one between two women, which might be safer for a lone girl.

Stretching toward the window in the coach door, she extended her hand and he took it. "I thank you for your care of me. How would I have managed?"

"You would not have," he said bluntly, but smiling. "Come back soon."

"It is only for a month or two, unless—"

The horn sounded.

"Soon!" he repeated fervently.

Their hands were torn apart by the plunge of horses.

As she shrank back into her proper place, Clio turned her attention to her traveling companions and discovered that the three opposite—two elderly gentlemen, shabby but respectable, and a rosy-cheeked woman with a fat round bundle on her lap—were beaming at her.

"Husband?" asked the woman.

"Oh, no."

"Well, then, *fee-an-cee?*"

Clio was astonished to be asked such a personal question, yet she felt obliged to clear matters. "Only a friend—a neighbor."

"Like to be more, I daresay, ducks," said one of the women beside her. This one, she saw now, was dressed in a shocking shade of green and appeared to have *paint* on her face.

At this point the gentleman with a gray mustache cleared his throat violently and the subject died.

For a young lady to be traveling alone was obviously not suitable, but of course trying to explain her situation would not help matters. Clio straightened to a very severe position, as if unapproachable, and endeavored to shrink herself from contact with her seatmates. With the swaying of the stagecoach this was not possible, nor did holding her breath help. She dreaded turning her head for a closer glance at either lady.

By the time they had reached the outskirts of the city and were bowling along more rapidly, Clio was relieved to see the three persons opposite were napping like longtime travelers. She could examine them more closely and be thankful that they, at least, seemed harmless. The man by the window was thick and dark with a Belcher scarf tied loosely about his neck. Now and then he smacked his lips and snorted, though he did not appear to wake up. She imagined he had a "head" from last night's indulgence and felt no interest in a prim young woman.

About the woman with the parcel, seated by the other window and riding placidly backward, she wasn't sure. She might not be sleeping at all, only pretending, for her hands continued to hold the strange bundle in a firm grip. Clio amused herself by imagining it was a *head* being transported to some shameful destination, until she noticed that the woman's hands were careworn as if she had long grubbed among vegetables and her face was prematurely lined, yet kind.

Just because she, Clio, had set off on an adventure of some sort, did not mean all the world was sinister! Besides, Gray Mustache, whose throat-clearing had been so dignified, was dozing now in a gentle and impeccable manner, keeping his mouth neatly closed and making no sound at all.

To sit stiffly as if she had swallowed a poker was far from comfortable. She was beginning to have a pain in her jaw from being rigid and her toes were numb.

From the corner of her eye she could see that the Green Woman was sagging as though asleep. Clio's back began to protest the poker, so she risked a sideways peek at the passenger on her right and met a conspiratorial glance of merry brown eyes.

"You cannot ride all the way to Bath like a stone statue," whispered the lady, whose hair was snow-white and whose pretty pink face was unlined except for crinkles at the outer corners of her eyes. She looked plump and friendly and kind.

Clio sighed, relaxing. "You do understand?"

"I do," answered the lady softly. "If my granddaughter had not sprained her ankle last evening she would be traveling with me today. *You* can be she, if you like. How far are you going?"

"To Scudderfield, ma'am."

"Well, I am to go all the way to Bath, so I will see you safely to your destination. Close your eyes and see whether you can sleep, my dear. Depend upon Mrs. Ames to keep watch."

Feeling very immature for someone who passed herself off as a companion, but thankful to have found Mrs. Ames who would not allow her to make any blunders, Clio did as she was bid and soon was dreaming of a similar lady whose name was Mary Linville.

A slowing of the coach, an abrupt turn left, and a stop threw Clio against her new friend and woke her rudely. The coachyard boiled with activity as the team was unhitched and fresh horses led out.

"Twenty minutes, loidies un gents!" bawled a voice.

Already the men were leaping to the ground as the four women gathered their cloaks and reticules, preparing to follow. The rosy woman was still clutching her odd package.

"Hurry, girl. We may get a swallow of coffee."

It was then that Clio saw Mrs. Ames was struggling

with a cane. "Oh," she exclaimed, "do you need
help?"

"Shush!" whispered the lady, "it is camouflage."

Sure enough, as they entered the coffee room last
of all, a place was made for Mrs. Ames and the girl by
Gray Mustache and coffee placed before them.

Clio found the coffee was just what she needed to
revive her. It was steaming and fragrant, but—alas!—
scalded her tongue. The men of their party seemed
to have throats of steel, for they poured down the
drink and held out their cups for more, but none of
the ladies could do that. The clock on the mantel, Clio
noticed anxiously, was nearing the nine-minute mark
before she could manage more than a few sips.

"Be calm, child," advised Mrs. Ames. "We can take
a little longer. They are having a spot of trouble."

Nothing could be seen. A great deal of ruckus could
be heard—quarreling voices, stamping of hooves, jingle of harnesses. One voice roared above the others:
"Confound it! Won't do!"

"That will indubitably be our driver," said Gray
Mustache.

"Is one horse too wild?" asked Clio nervously.

"No, no. More likely it is a slug and he will not accept such a creature. Would throw the whole team
off."

"Who will prevail?"

"Our driver, of course, unless there isn't another
animal. Ah, now! I believe there is. Drink your coffee
quickly, miss."

The tumult had died. Presently the horn sounded
and they hurried outside. It amused Clio to see everyone stand back for Mrs. Ames, with her cane, to board
first.

"You see," murmured Mrs. Ames aside to Clio.
"The cane does the trick, but only, to be sure, if there

is a gentleman present. I think we have one—or two—today."

Everyone had revived, even the man in the Belcher tie. He wiped his hand across his jaw and mouth. "Could have used another cup," he volunteered. His voice sounded educated, which surprised Clio, although she knew next to nothing about drink and indulgers. Her father had once said that sometimes even gentlemen overdid.

Gray Mustache offered mildly, "Food will do you more good. At our next stop we may be offered a meal of sorts."

There was a murmur of agreement and approval.

Mrs. Ames and the rosy woman began to chat. "You have been holding that bundle so long and must need a rest," Mrs. Ames said. "Why not put it on the floor between our feet? I am sure we can make room."

"Oh, I couldn't! That is, thank you for the suggestion, but it is my treasure—the teapot I always wanted."

"Teapot!" exclaimed Clio involuntarily.

"Yes. A dear Dresden one that I may never dare to use and may keep sitting prettily on the dresser."

Clio smiled and nodded as if she understood the sentiment, inwardly she rebuked herself for her wild speculations.

Meanwhile, Mrs. Ames and the woman drifted into a mild discussion of teas, while other passengers stared lazily at passing meadows.

At the next stop they did, indeed, obtain food—crusty meat pasties hot from the oven that were very good. Unfortunately, at this station Gray Mustache left them and his place was taken by a Young Blood who was bored until he found amusement in ogling Clio. He even went so far as to press the toe of her slipper with a glossy, white-capped boot.

Mortified, she tucked back both feet in an uncom-

fortable manner, looking anxiously to Mrs. Ames who
said in the voice of Pallas Athene: "Would you like to
have the window seat for a change, dearest?"

Without waiting for Clio's answer, she announced
that she would stand so that Clio could slip under her
and she would then drop into the center seat. In a
rollicking coach it was not a simple maneuver, yet such
was Mrs. Ames's confidence and Clio's eagerness and
the coach's cooperation in swerving that both ladies
fell exactly into place.

The would-be lothario, being young enough and
inexperienced enough to be embarrassed, resumed a
bored expression and turned his attention to the
gaudy female on the other side of Mrs. Ames. She appeared to have been enjoying the whole episode and
now batted her lashes in hopes of some entertainment
on a tedious drive. He reacted immediately, expand-
ing himself somehow in a mysterious manner.

The four other passengers watched with interest.
The woman was handsome, in a coarse sort of way,
and her speech was not refined, though generally
grammatical. Except for Clio, it was probable none of
the viewers supposed she had any real interest in the
youth.

"You must excuse me for being personal, sir, but I
do admire your waistcoat—such an unusual blend of
colors," she purred.

The young man's chest expanded visibly and his
coat parted further to reveal more of the interesting
garment.

"Meaky. Fellow I found in London. Does smashing
work," he replied happily, his voice rising in pitch as
he continued. "Sure to set a fashion."

"Yes, indeed," she said. "You are certain to start a
new style."

Clio, whose knowledge of men's fashions was next
to nothing, thought privately that it was a very odd

waistcoat, a bold sort of flame stitch in purple, holly red, and orange.

"You must be sure to tell your friends in London about this—Meaky?" the woman admonished.

He shifted uneasily. "Well, as to that, I am not very well—er—acquainted in London, but my friends at Oxf—my friends at home will be *green,* although what my parents will say," his voice faltered, "I don't know."

With a straight face, the woman said, "You must tell them it is all the crack. I expect they have confidence in your taste."

A blow to their confidence, Clio thought. She exchanged a look with Mrs. Ames who nodded slightly, keeping a solemn countenance. Clio's lips twitched. She turned her face away and stared purposefully at undulating farmland. Somehow it did not seem as colorful as it had before, in comparison with the garish waistcoat. No. There was less light to sparkle colors. The sun had gone behind a cloud. A glance upward revealed gathering clouds that were dark and threatening.

"It is going to rain!" she exclaimed.

There were assorted assents as everyone craned to see what the sky had to offer.

"The road will be a quagmire," groaned the man in the Belcher tie. "I know this stretch."

"No saying when we will reach home," said the woman with the teapot, looking glum. Her face remained rosy, however, proving it was wind and weather that had marked her, not disposition.

Mrs. Ames told them she knew the area well from having traveled it many times. "I think the rain may hold off until we reach those hills ahead, but the road will be difficult there. We will be lucky if I am wrong."

It soon became evident that she was not wrong at all.

Raindrops began to spatter casually, not enough to

make the coachman turn up his collar, though. What made him curse to himself was something he could see which the travelers could not: a large, lumbering, loaded fourgon pulled by four sturdy workhorses. The heavy vehicle just ahead, occupied two-thirds of the road and moved slowly. Fortunately, he was able to check his team before crashing into it. Even if the fourgon pulled perilously close to the ditch, there would be no room for a stagecoach to pass. It was the stuff of coachmen's nightmares. At least he was not driving the mail with a tight schedule. Cursing would not help. Nor sounding the horn. The torrent Mrs. Ames had predicted began to fall. Visibility was rotten.

Inside the coach the travelers felt the loss of speed. Soon they were deafened by water pounding on the roof.

"It will be downhill soon," Mrs. Ames said.

"Yes," agreed the man with the Belcher tie. "I can feel the slope already, and it will become steeper."

"We are into the hills now," added Clio. "I can just see rounded gray blobs."

"Well," said Mrs. Ames in heartening manner, "let us thank heaven that we have a cautious driver. Some would be racing through the mud which can be dangerously slick."

For a few minutes the stage continued to advance slowly. Then it slued abruptly and came to a safe halt. The ladies squealed. Almost immediately a guard appeared at the door and shouted through the noise of the downpour that the road was blocked. "Sit tight. No danger. We'll see—"

He vanished into the obscuring rainfall.

"Good God!" exclaimed the man with the Belcher tie. He hastily struggled into his cloak, which had been wadded as an armrest under one elbow, and, to everyone's astonishment, hurled himself out the door.

"Now *there* is a man with energy. Not the rounder

that he seemed," observed Mrs. Ames, turning to Clio. "Would you say a good yeoman on his way home from a dash to the metropolis?"

"My opinion is worthless, ma'am. The only men with whom I have any contact are scholarly gentlemen and shopkeepers. Do you think he will be of any help with the problem?"

"Depends on what it is. Not likely to be brigands in this weather, I think."

The Young Blood across the aisle asked diffidently whether they wished him to see if he could discover the problem.

Four pairs of female eyes fastened on him and having assessed his exquisite attire, youthfulness, and lack of ease, all, in a mingling of protests, said no, no, he must not think of it.

Mrs. Ames kindly added that they would feel a deal more comfortable to have his company.

Not long after that the guard returned, his shoulders black where the water had soaked his coat. He reported that a wagon had skidded sideways, blocking the road. Nothing was broken, though part of the load had toppled into the mud. They would have to reload before the wagon could be moved. "The horses are edgy, but the gentulmun what was with you is doin' a marvel at calming 'em." He addressed himself to the remaining male traveler. "Pardon, sir. Think you could hold our team whilst the driver helps with the loading?" To which the aspiring Young Blood replied, "Yes, I think I could do that."

"Gracious!" cried Clio. "He will spoil his clothes! And the white tops of his fine boots."

As if uncertain whether to be glad to be defended by a pretty girl or mortified by his own unusefulness, the young gentleman stammered, "B-boots don't matter."

"Then come along, sir," growled the guard. "If we don' get to woik we'll be 'ere till tomorrow."

"Oh, not that long," interrupted a voice, as the man with the Belcher tie appeared beside them. "The farm horses are quiet enough now, so the farmer's lad can hold them. No need to drench this fellow, too. Ladies, this is going to take some time. After the fourgon is loaded, we still must turn the vehicle to its course, and may have to unhitch the team to do it. At any rate, you can keep dry here." As a fresh downpour descended he added, "Good God! Will this never end?" and sloshed away in the gloom.

Mrs. Ames consulted the watch pinned to her bosom. "After three. Might as well be night from the looks of things. We are going to be late at the next change and later still at Scudderfield."

Clio looked troubled. "Mrs. Linville will think I did not come. Her carriage won't wait for me."

"Nonsense. The groom she sends will certainly learn that your stage is behind schedule. Scudderfield is not a change station, so we will only be there long enough to drop your trunk and pop you out, but I shall call to the host—that's Barney Brill—to take care of you. Mustn't worry."

Warming to Mrs. Ames's affirmative spirit, the young man explained that he, too, was being met at the next change. "The Pater won't like waiting. Impatient, don't you know? Might even be anxious."

"Splendid!" retorted Mrs. Ames. As the youth stared at her open-mouthed, she continued: "The more anxious he grows, the gladder he will be to find you undamaged."

"By George! Is it possible?" He looked to Clio for confirmation and she nodded.

"Yes, it is possible," said Mrs. Ames, "but I cannot guarantee the reception of your waistcoat."

The four ladies laughed. He looked chagrined and therefore more human.

Those who could do so napped. The rain continued

unabated, and presumably the surface of the highway became muddier. Although there were occasional buffets of wind which rocked the coach, there was no thunder or lightning, for which all were grateful.

No one complained.

No traffic piled up behind them.

They could see nothing of the work ahead.

This was one occasion when it was convenient to be a female, Clio thought, yawning with boredom. It was dark enough for night. She tucked her head against one shoulder and drifted, semiconscious, wondering why the coachman had not turned their carriage and sought another route. She supposed this was not possible. *I am getting horridly bedraggled and will not be welcome at Scudderfield,* she thought. It was comforting to remember that she had enough money for a return trip, if she needed it. Instinctively, she held her reticule closer, like the farm woman with her Dresden teapot.

Across the way, the Young Blood had moved to the vacant seat and was slumped against the window. He eyed the garish woman opposite as if seeking to revive amusing conversation with her, but got no cooperation, as she was snoring with a faint little wheezing, tinkling sound.

The sudden opening of the coach door to admit the man with a sodden Belcher tie aroused everyone. "Done," he said, falling into the empty center seat and mopping his face imperfectly with the tie.

"Will we go on now?" asked Clio.

"Not immediately, miss," he answered. "It all depends if the fourgon can climb the hill ahead. Our driver says we can do it if the blasted wagon doesn't stall again. There is a freshet at the dip and it's running fast, but it's not deep." Seeing the ladies' anxious faces he added, "Now, now, ladies, you'll get across, if I have to carry each one of you. There now, isn't that a fair promise?"

"You have been splendid, sir," Clio declared.

He gave a challenging glance at the youth on his right.

"Well, I expect this gentleman will give me some help."

"C-certainly," the young man said courageously. At the prospect of finally getting under way, he had brightened.

It seemed ages that they had to sit unmoving, although the man explained that they had to be sure when the fourgon had cleared the hill before their own horses could safely lunge for the climb.

"How can our coachman *see* in all this rain and darkness?" asked Clio. She seemed to be the only one with questions; of course, it was her first journey and she was apprehensive.

"He can see enough. And he can hear the squeal of the dratted wagon. Besides, the rain is easing up."

It was true, as all discovered when they rubbed the windows and peeked out. Suddenly there was a jerk, signaling the guard had jumped aboard, and the coach moved forward, gathering momentum as it descended the remainder of the downhill run. It churned safely across the rivulet and charged uphill with all passengers taking a deep breath to assist their horses in the climb.

"After five," observed Mrs. Ames. "Dear me, we are later than I would have expected. Well, from now on the course is easier. We should be at the next changing station in forty-five minutes. No, with this mud perhaps we should expect an hour."

"Aye," agreed the man in the ruined Belcher tie.

The estimate was close. At not quite six they swung into the change yard. The rain was intermittent, but skies were still forbidding. While the coachman examined one of his team which had kicked its own leg and ordered care of all his animals, the travelers thankfully stepped down to seek shelter in the low, sprawling hostelry.

With her cane, Mrs. Ames of course came last. "Look, dear. The vain young man has met his papa."

They were in time to see a distinguished man with a handsome white mane and a very elegant drab coat. He seized and embraced his son, then stood back to look him over. They heard him say, "My God!"

"A-all the crack," stammered the youth.

"Crack? Well, don't let your mother see you like that."

Giggling, the ladies scampered indoors.

When the horn sounded departure it was discovered that the man with the Belcher scarf had gone his own way, so only the four ladies remained to continue the journey. All felt damp, mussed, and not inclined to chatter. It was well after seven before they reached Scudderfield.

This village was a small one which looked somewhat forlorn with almost deserted streets. Not many lights showed, since most curtains were drawn snugly. There was a darkened church with a stone-walled graveyard and ghostly hulks of laurel, but no inn or posting house that Clio could see.

"The inn is across the river," Mrs. Ames explained.

No river was visible either, yet presently they felt tremors as the coach rumbled across a wooden bridge and pulled right into an innyard.

So seldom did the Bath stage stop here that the arrival of one at a late hour brought Master Brill himself to his door. Indeed, even before Mrs. Ames had called to him, he had sprung forward swiftly for such a heavy man and yanked open the carriage door.

"Ladies! 'Pon my soul!" he bellowed. "All ladies!"

"Only one for you, Barney Brill," said Mrs. Ames
sternly. "You remember me, I presume?"

"Aye. Mrs. Ames from Bath. Could I forget?"

"Better not." She motioned to Clio who rose hastily.
"This young *lady* is expected by the Linvilles. Step
down, dear. Take care of her, Barney, until they come
for her. Should be here already."

"No one's here," he answered, lifting Clio bodily
from the coach. "We've just had a nasty storm."

Clio's trunk landed with a thump.

"Mrs. Brill and I will keep her safe until someone
comes from the Hall." He drew the girl back from the
way of splatters as a whip cracked and the stagecoach
spun away into deepening dark.

"Good-bye!" she called. "Thank you!" To Master
Brill she added, "Such a kind lady."

"Aye. The best," he agreed. "This way, miss."

Inside the timbered inn, ancient and cosy, was Mrs.
Brill, who clucked sympathetically and took Clio in
charge as a mother might have done. She was as small
as her spouse was large, though she was in no way
intimidated by him. Concern showed in her eyes, and
her spanking clean apron inspired confidence. Clio
did not know much about the *haut monde,* but she
could recognize solid worth.

"Would you be liking a good wash, miss?" asked
Mrs. Brill.

"I would like it of all things," Clio replied fervently.
She did not want to mention supper because she
feared it would compel this kind woman to insist on
giving her some. Clio had money to pay, but did not
wish either to insult by offering cash or to offend by
rejecting generosity. Mrs. Brill led her to her own
pleasant chamber, helped to remove her cloak and
bonnet, and produced a fleecy white towel, soap, and
a basin of warm water.

While Clio removed the ravages of travel as best she

could, Mrs. Brill kept up a gentle spiel about the recent spell of wet weather.

"It has rained most of the day," she said. "Only ceased about an hour before you arrived. I expect the winds were moving the clouds your way."

Clio explained, "We were caught behind a wagon on a very bad hill."

"Oh, yes. I daresay that was Nevermore Hill."

Clio laughed and said indeed she nevermore wanted to wait there again. "I fear Mrs. Linville's carriage did not wait here for *me*, so I must cast myself upon you. Can you tell me how to proceed next?"

Mrs. Brill took away the damp towel and watched while Clio tidied her hair. "Why, as to that, we will ask Master Brill. If Mrs. Linville's carriage was here at any time he will know. There may be some message for you, miss."

Barney Brill, when applied to, said that no carriage had come since the mail passed at noon. "Are ye sure 'twas today that was meant?"

"I cannot be mistaken. Mrs. Linville wrote to say for me to come to Scudderfield on Friday, and although we sat forever in the middle of a storm, I cannot think this can be Saturday."

"Right ye are. Now, Mrs. Linville, did you say? Which Mrs. Linville? Was it Mr. Roland's wife?"

"I don't know. She signed herself 'Mary Linville.' "

Brill's face lighted up and his wife had begun to smile and nod. "Ah," said Brill, "you mean *Lady* Linville. Well, if she was expecting you and was supposed to send her carriage, then something must have happened."

"Yes, yes, Barney Brill," said his wife, "but the young lady cannot wait here while we speculate about happenings." To Clio she added, "We are not actually in Scudderfield, being just across the little river, but there isn't another inn in the village—she did say 'inn'?—so you must have come to the right place. Mr. Brill will take you to the dower house. It's only a mile or two, and no traffic on the lane at this hour. Barney will drive you in the whiskey, won't you, Barney Brill?"

"Aye," agreed Master Brill heavily.

"But I cannot let you," protested Clio. "The mud—your poor horse—the dark!"

As soon as he was told he mustn't, Master Brill appeared to decide he must. "Aw, old Cottle hasn't been out all day and he likes mud as well as straw."

Clio said weakly, "The dark—"

"Many's the times I've tied a lantern on his collar so he could see where to set his feet," declared Mr. Brill. "Besides, I know the lanes about here like the lines in my palms."

"Hitch up," commanded Mrs. Brill. "There won't be customers here tonight."

Three

It was fully dark by the time Barney Brill and Clio set out from the inn, recrossing the wooden bridge to Scudderfield and turning left to follow the stream northward along a gently winding lane. Dense clouds shut off light from moon or stars, but clever Barney had hung a lantern from Cottle's collar, which the animal did not seem to mind at all. He had also hung lanterns on each side of the whiskey, placing them low enough to cast light left and right without blinding the passengers. Clio could see shaggy bushes and intermittent trees along the invisible river. To the right a hill grew gradually steeper, until it became a rough cliff.

No wind blew, which probably explained the lingering cloud cover. There was little sound except a soft jingle of harness and a low sort of whistle from between Mr. Brill's teeth as he drove Cottle at a lackadaisical walk.

Drove? It seemed to Clio that Mr. Brill merely held the reins loosely while Cottle proceeded as he pleased. The whole trip seemed very odd, though not unpleasant.

"Mr. Brill," she said at last, "did you say that Mrs. Linville is a *Lady*?" The London journals wrote about Lady This or That, and countesses and duchesses, a few of whom Clio had seen, without ever meeting. Papa was gently born and likewise Mrs. Mellow; nei-

ther had any acquaintance with nobility and very little
curiosity about them.

"That she is," he replied. "A fine, kind lady. Been
a widow for five years."

"And did you say you would take me to the dower
house?"

"Aye. Mrs. Linville's stepson, young Sir Malcolm
Linville, lives in the Hall now. Mrs. Linville had the
raising of him and he thinks the world of her. Offered
her a whole wing to herself if she would stay, but she
said it wasn't fair to young Lady Linville. Moved body
and kin to the dower house."

"Oh. Are there other children?"

"Three."

Clio gnawed her lip. "Do you suppose she really
wanted a governess? I thought I was to be a companion
for her!"

"Of course she doesn't mean governess," asserted
Mr. Brill. "They are all grown. What puzzles me is why
she would need a companion with so many people
around. Even the family butler moved to the dower
house . . . proud old fellow, though not up to much
work. Matter of fact, he's my wife's father, and I must
say he took it hard when she set her mind to marry
me. Didn't like the idea of her fillin' mugs, don't you
know? Well, I got her, all right, and the old fellow is
mighty glad to have our daughter, Maybelle, to be
nurse for Mr. Roland's three young ones. Thinks that's
a proper station for *her*."

When he paused to take a breath, Clio quickly said:
"So many people! So confusing. Which of Mrs. Linville's children will I find?"

"Three, like I said," grumbled Mr. Brill, while enjoying himself. "Miss Eleanor is the oldest, then Mr.
Roland, and Mr. Halloran who is home for a visit. You
are goin' to have to look out for Mr. Hal, missy. Up to
every rig and row. He sets all the village girls a-flutter.

Not, I mean to say, that he sedu . . . plays fast and loose with any. But a horrid tease, I guess you might say. A girl could get hurt. Understand?"

Clio nodded, only partly understanding. "Thank you, Mr. Brill. I don't think a baronet's son will take any interest in his mother's *companion.*"

"Anything in skirts," growled Mr. Brill. "Hello! What's that ahead?"

The cliff had squeezed the lane closer to the river. It reared starkly now, the top out of sight in the darkness. At the base several lanterns glowed, spreading a yellowish semicircle upon the rock wall.

Cottle's pace was so slow that Clio had time to count four lanterns. There was nothing else. It did seem peculiar that anyone would leave four lanterns bravely burning in the middle of nowhere.

"A poor sort of prank," muttered Barney Brill. "Foolery—and not even All Hallows Eve or Guy Fawkes Day."

As the whiskey carried them farther, the cliff slid away until it vanished, out of the reach of their own lights. Presently, a driveway appeared on the right, and Mr. Brill turned Cottle between stone posts capped with benign, seated lions. There were shadowy trees and shrubs to create a dream setting, although Clio could not identify the species.

"Seems sort of ghostly and forgotten," she murmured.

"This is the home farm entrance, but the closest way to the dower house," Brill answered.

As the climb became steeper Cottle cast back a mildly reproving glance before leaning into his collar. The pace continued steadily like that of a lazy turtle, and soon the many curves of the driveway made Clio lose all sense of direction. The sky was not visible. She thought they must be moving northeast.

When the trees parted on the right, and a few lights

glimmered through the foliage, she assumed they were nearing their destination, so she exclaimed, "Is this the dower house?"

Mr. Brill said, "No. This is Mr. Roland's cottage. We are almost there, though."

After another curve, they emerged to a level graveled area and were facing a house of which few details could be discerned except that the front door stood half-open.

Brill swung to a stop and handed Clio the reins.

"Will you hold these, miss, while I set down your trunk and try to find a servant?" he said.

As Cottle was already half-asleep, his shoulders slumped, she accepted the lines without a murmur.

Mr. Brill, being a powerful man, easily hoisted her small trunk and carried it up a few steps to the entry, where he sounded the knocker first modestly and then imperatively. There was no response. "Hulloo," he boomed. Setting the trunk beside the door, he returned to Clio.

"I mislike to go in, miss," he said, "but I think you could, seeing as how you're expected."

To enter boldly the house of a baronet's widow without being welcomed was the last thing Clio could imagine daring to do. She thundered the knocker, called "Hello!", knocked again and longer, and finally called "Hello!" in an abused tone of voice. She looked back to Barney Brill, who hunched his shoulders.

Beginning to be annoyed, she muttered, "This is ridiculous. Do I go in?"

Mr. Brill said, "Yes."

"Are you sure this is the right place?"

"In course, I'm sure. Don't I deliver ale here regular? Don't my pa-in-law work here? You can bet I'll rag him about this!"

While Mr. Brill watched, holding Cottle's reins casually, Clio advanced into the hall of the house, calling, "Hello? Hello? Anyone here?"

There was a lighted lamp in the hallway, making the tan flags of the floor glow warmly and a straight oak stairway gleam until it vanished into the shadows of a second floor. To the left three lamps were lit in what appeared to be an elegant drawing room with portraits watching from walls of green damask.

Dare she sit to wait?

Clio stepped back to the entry, dragged her trunk within, and waved Barney Brill off. She watched while he woke Cottle with a slap of lines and wheeled the whiskey away. After that, she closed the door and entered the drawing room to explore. She was poised to leap to the entrance again if necessary. She hoped to be able to give the appearance of having just arrived.

What would Papa have said about daring to enter uninvited? Surely, he would not expect his daughter to shiver on the doorstep until someone should come! He would be distressed about her situation—in or out. Mrs. Mellow, she thought, would say indignantly that these people deserved invasion for neglecting an invited guest. She must enter!

Well, she had. So she might as well sit somewhere.

In the drawing room twin graceful open-arm chairs with cream upholstery flanked a mantel within which an unlit fire was laid Her eyes swept a marketry table, an apricot sofa, and more exquisite ornaments than she could count. Her eyes moved on to a doorway in the rear wall; its pair of doors stood open to reveal a dining parlor.

The remarkable thing, here, was that dishes and silver were littered upon the table, serviettes flung down helter-skelter, and chairs thrust back. Everything pointed to a sudden interruption of a meal. White tapers still burned in tall, crystal holders. She guessed, from the wax that had dripped on the cloth, that the candles had been lit for quite some time.

"I have walked into a fairy tale," she whispered to herself. "What does it mean?"

At this point, the entrance door abruptly opened, and a male voice exclaimed, "Good God! A trunk! Don't fall over it, Eleanor. Careful, Helen."

Heart thudding, Clio sped down the drawing room to confront two ladies, a stunning gentleman, and a small boy. They stared at her with white faces.

"I beg your pardon," she gasped. "I knocked and knocked but no one came. The door was open, so Mr. Brill brought my trunk into . . ."

"Who are you?" demanded the younger woman. She had a sharp face and angry, piercing eyes.

"Miss Caldicott," replied Clio, becoming calmer as she became more indignant herself. "Are you Mrs. Linville who wrote to me?"

"I am Mrs. Linville but I certainly did not write to any Miss Caldicott!"

"Come, Eleanor," said the man to the older woman who was dabbing her eyes with a sodden handkerchief. She was rather pretty in a colorless way. "Let Helen handle this. We need to choose clothes."

"Oh, Hal, we needn't do that yet!" she protested.

"I want to get it over," he insisted. "Come along, Elly." He prodded her toward the staircase.

Watching, Clio said, "Now I understand." She turned back to the angry lady, adding, "You must be Mrs. Roland Linville."

The woman nodded impatiently.

"Lady Mary Linville—your mother-in-law, is she not?—wrote asking me to come to her while the lady I attend was out of town. She said she had need of a companion."

"That is preposterous!" cried Helen Linville. "Lady Linville, in the bosom of her devoted family, would never have need of a companion. Why, there is scarcely a moment that one or two of us are not here in the house. You can't get away with such an excuse to worm yourself into this household."

Clio felt tears start in her eyes. No one had ever addressed her so angrily and so crudely. She drew herself up and said with measured words, "Lady Linville wrote 'I am in need of a companion, myself.' "

Mrs. Linville extended her palm. "Let me see the letter."

Hoping to hide her dismay, Clio replied that Mrs. Mellow had accidently gone off to York with the letter in her trunk.

"Likely story," snapped Mrs. Linville. "What sort of name is Mellow? Eleanor will have to settle this. I have no patience with . . . oh, sit somewhere," she added, flinging herself toward the stairs.

Clio walked unsteadily into the drawing room and sank onto the nearest chair, only to find the lad had followed her and was standing anxiously before her.

"Gammy's dead," he said tremulously, tears welling from his eyes.

"Oh dear heaven," she whispered. The trouble of her own situation seemed nothing compared to this child's grief. She seized the boy and enfolded him in her arms. Where was his mother? Which was his mother? Helen, of course, because he had the same dark hair and eyes . . . although his nature was tenderer. She burned with indignation, as she groped with one hand for a handkerchief.

His sobs were tapering off. When, presently, he drew away and smiled adoringly at her, Clio gently mopped his face and asked cautiously what had happened.

"She fell from the cliff," he answered. There was a crack in his voice, but tears were gone.

The flares in the lane, Clio thought, did have meaning. A horrid, tragic meaning.

"I love Gammy," he said next.

"I'm sure she loved you. It is something you can always, always remember. Do you want me to find your mama?"

"No. I want my May," he replied, endeavoring to climb upon her lap.

"May?" she asked. "May! Do you mean Maybelle Brill?"

He nodded. "May loves me. She says so."

"And so do I," declared Clio promptly. "Shall we look for May? Where shall we look?"

The child led her into the dining salon and through an inconspicuous door to what was plainly a service pantry. From a steep half-stair, to the head of which the boy trotted, rose the faint exchange of doleful conversation.

"May—ee!" cried the child.

There was the noise of a chair or stool being upset. A warm voice exclaimed, "That's my Teddy! I'm comin', darlin'."

They met on the stair in a great, wide, wonderful hug, Teddy going down three steps and Maybelle coming up five. Over the boy's head Maybelle looked up in surprise at a stranger.

"I am Miss Caldicott," said Clio quickly, "here for a visit. Such a difficult moment. May I leave Teddy with you? His mother is somewhere above."

"Oh, yes, miss," responded the bonny nursemaid with a smile. She looked sweet and clean, with the same clear brown eyes and round cheeks as her mother. "Teddy is my charge. Come along, darlin'. We will go home to bed." She led young Master Linville down the remaining steps and out of Clio's view. There was the sound of a door opening, and soon closing.

Clio heard nothing more from whatever servants remained in the kitchen. She sighed, then returned to find a seat in the drawing room as she had been told. Passing through the dining salon, she hesitated a moment to examine the table more closely. It had been set for eight. At one place there was a smaller plate with a child's silver mug beside it, and a spoon on the floor below. Teddy, surely.

Two places were untouched. Had Lady Linville not been at dinner? That would explain one at the head of the table. But if so, why had she not attended the meal? Out for a walk on an evening that had been damp and gloomy, if not actually stormy? Still, there remained one unused seat. Had it been intended for *her*? In that case, would not her name have been mentioned? Yet they had been surprised to see her—or had forgotten. It was very strange.

She continued to the drawing room and chose a chair closest to the hall doorway where they would be sure to see her. Her trunk waited forlornly in the hall. She wondered what was to become of her after this. She would be obliged to sleep here one night—unless they sent her back to the inn. She was certainly a nuisance in the Linvilles' time of trouble!

During the time she had been with Teddy and Maybelle, Mrs. Linville and Mr. Hal Linville must have departed, for she never saw them again that night. Helen Linville surely had to go home sometime, although Hal could have shut himself in his room.

Not only tired, but also bored, Clio gazed about the drawing room and wondered about the nature of the lady who had chosen such beautiful colors and furnishings. A lady of exquisite taste, she thought.

Over the mantel was a portrait of a distinguished man, hair just beginning to turn gray. His eyes were direct and wise, Clio decided. It seemed likely that it was a portrait of the late Sir Linville that should have remained at the Hall. Perhaps Lady Linville had commissioned and paid for it herself. Was there a companion portrait of Lady Linville? Not in this room, nor in the dining parlor.

At last steps sounded gently on the main stair, and Clio rose to her feet as Eleanor came into the room.

"Miss—?"

"Caldicott," supplied Clio quickly.

Eleanor nodded slightly. "Miss Caldicott," she said in a soft, controlled, colorless voice, "we do not understand. Did my mother write to you and ask you to come for a visit?"

"Not to me, ma'am," corrected Clio. "She wrote to Mrs. Mellow, with whom I have been making my home. Mrs. Mellow has gone for a stay with her son in York, and Lady Linville asked for me to come to her during the interim. I was to take the stage to Scudderfield on Friday—today—and she would arrange to have someone meet me."

"It seems very curious," said Eleanor in an uncritical manner. "She told none of us. And no one met you?"

"The stage was two hours late," Clio explained. "I thought perhaps you assumed that the stage would not reach here tonight. Mr. Brill brought me to the house in his whiskey."

Eleanor made a "tisk" noise with her tongue. "Well," she allowed, "there is no way to settle this so late. I am Lady Linville's daughter, Mrs. Hampden. Come with me. I will find a bed for you."

"My trunk—" reminded Clio apologetically.

"Someone will bring it," Eleanor said vaguely as she began to climb the stairs. Clio followed, reluctant but obedient. "It is not a large house, you see," continued Eleanor. "Edward and our son Mark and I moved in with Mama to make room in the cottage for Roland's family when it grew in size three years ago. Roland and Helen have three children now." She paused at the head of the stairs and gestured to three doors facing them on a wide landing. "We occupy these three rooms. Mama's sitting room is—was over the Gold Salon at the front of the house, with her bedchamber on beyond, over the library. My brother Hal, of course, has his room across from Mama's sitting room. Here is another hall, you see, crossing between my room and my brother's to reach the service steps."

They halted here, and Clio saw that a flight came up on the left from the serving pantry that she had visited with Teddy. By the steps were a series of cupboards. Eleanor opened one, from which she took sheets and a towel, and handed them to Clio. "I hope you will excuse our not having a room prepared for you. This is only a small one. The other is shared by two maids."

Clio murmured something indistinguishable and followed her hostess into the room on the right. A lamp in the hall gave enough light for Mrs. Hampden to see to ignite a candle. Clio was relieved to discover the chamber was considerably larger than a servant's quarters and nearly as large and charming as her room at Mrs. Mellow's. The walls were a clean, fresh white and there were two windows curtained in a rose-sprinkled chintz.

"I will send up your trunk and some warm water," promised Eleanor. "Please forgive our inhospitality at a sorrowful time. My mother has fallen—died." After a pause she added, "Early breakfast—eight, I suppose."

Clio gulped, "Good night," as the door closed.

She sank upon the bed, her emotions a mixture of chagrin, loneliness, hunger, remorse, and pity. She felt fortunate that the Linvilles had not cast her off without explanation.

Perhaps most of all she felt exhausted from her long journey. The first thing in order, therefore, was to make up the bed. She sprang to her feet and drew down the counterpane. There to her astonished eyes appeared a rosy blanket and pristine sheets, sweet with the aroma of fresh *potpourri*.

She *had* been expected by Lady Linville!

At this point she heard steps in the hall, followed by a light knock. She opened the door. A footman and a maid entered, bearing her trunk and hot water. Their faces had a closed look. It was impossible to read their sentiments, though she suspected an honest grief.

As soon as they had gone away, Clio stripped, washed, and dived into her night dress. The bed looked inviting. She nipped between the covers, flinching from the touch of cool linen, but she was warmed rapidly by the pretty blanket.

It had been the most astonishing and tiring day! She felt as though she had aged years, due to the odd and disturbing events crowded into about fifteen hours. Until now, she had never realized how protected her life had been with sweet Papa and dear Mrs. Mellow.

Today the physician's apprentice had taught her how kind and respectful a young gentleman could be, making no awkward advances when she was unchaperoned. The garish woman in the stage must have a kind heart, too, for she caused Clio no embarrassment after the gentleman with the gray mustache gave a hint. The farm woman was friendly in her way. As for Mrs. Ames, she was a godsend, protecting her from that encroaching young man. Even he turned out to be only a youth trying his wings. Perhaps most surprising of all was the man in the Belcher tie whom she had supposed to be a ne'er-do-well, a rounder, yet he was the one who ruined his clothes and spent his strength to help their coach over a bad place. It just proved, as Mr. Lambton sometimes preached, that a clean heart might be found inside a shoddy package.

She was not so certain about the Linville family. She was seeing them at a distressful time and could make no real appraisal. She positively hated imposing on them when they must wish her at Timbuktu. But there was no help for it. They were too well-bred to turn her away in the middle of the night, even if they doubted her story.

She could write to Mrs. Mellow for verification, of course, but they would want to be rid of her long before an answer could come. In any case, she did not belong here.

She had not met Mr. Hampden or Roland Linville. What they would decide about her, or what influence they would have in a decision, she did not know. She thought Halloran Linville was the most beautiful man she had ever seen—such liquid green eyes, such a mobile mouth, and broad shoulders. She fervently thanked Mr. Brill for his warning.

I suppose, she thought, these people must view me as a terrible nuisance at best, or a conniver at worst, or a mindless chit at least. Thank goodness I can go home. Home? She had no home, in the real sense. But she had Mrs. Mellow. Mr. Thatch would be glad to see her. He had said "come soon"—hadn't he?

A little smile played about her mouth.

But how hungry she was! It was good to know that breakfast would be early.

Four

The cautious footsteps of the maids crossing the landing woke Clio to dewy sunlight, the clouds having scudded away while she slept. No one remembered to bring fresh water, so she tidied herself with what remained from the night before.

What, she wondered, would be the most appropriate of her dresses? She selected a light blue muslin with a frill of white embroidery around the throat and long snug sleeves that buttoned at the wrist with tiny buttons. It seemed demure enough.

The awful thought then occurred that she could not fasten herself up in the back. No other of her frocks was suitable. And to meet any of the family half-clad would be shocking.

Meanwhile, tantalizing scents of coffee rose up the service stairway. Papa loved coffee, she remembered sadly.

Fastening the top button at the back of her neck to keep her dress from slipping off, she tiptoed oh so carefully across the landing and down the flight to the service pantry. No one was there, so she continued to creep down the half-flight to the kitchen.

The cook and two maids received her with astonishment, but soon realized what was needed.

"Thank you, thank you," she whispered. "I felt a perfect muffin-head. Don't tell!"

The younger maid, a homely girl with a mop of red

hair, protested, "Oh, miss! You must ring any time you need help."

Clio replied that she feared she was very much in the way and as welcome as a toothache.

The redhead said, "You're a guest, miss. I answer that bell." And Clio perceived that the girl would be offended if she were ignored.

"How good of you," she said warmly. "You will spoil me, I think, but I will appreciate your help." The cook and the second maid, a somewhat older woman, were both red-eyed, Clio noticed.

"Please let me say how sorry I am," she begged earnestly. "This is a very sad time for all of you. I did not know Lady Linville, but I can see you held her in deep affection."

"Oh, yes, miss," croaked Cook, dabbing her nose with her apron. "The best mistress in the world!"

The older maid, marked by flyaway brows above troubled eyes, burst out, "We thought she was napping in her room. It doesn't seem possible she could be out f-falling f-from the cl . . ." She clapped a hand violently over nose and mouth and sank onto the nearest stool.

Two years was not long enough for Clio to recover entirely from the death of her papa. Her own loss came rolling back like tides at the Solway. "I know," she whispered. "I'll slip upstairs now. Don't give me away. You must keep doing your best for your mistress—and Miss Eleanor."

She was able to reach her room undetected. After a quick check of her appearance in the mirror of her room, she took a deep breath and descended properly via the main staircase to the dining salon where the family was breakfasting. The house, being small, had no breakfast parlor.

Eleanor, still wan though no longer tearful, looked up from her seat at the foot of the table, to see Clio in the doorway. "Come in, Miss Caldicott. You haven't met my husband, Mr. Hampden."

The middle-aged gentleman on Eleanor's right lurched to his feet, saying, "Please sit here by me, young lady." Only five places were set. As the chair he indicated was at the only unoccupied place, Clio moved to take it.

"And this is my son, Mark," continued Eleanor, indicating the youth at her left who appeared interested chiefly in eating. When Clio acknowledged him, he only grunted.

Imperturbably Eleanor indicated the gentleman next to Mark. "You have met my brother, Mr. Linville."

"No, no," Halloran Linville objected. "We have only *encountered*. How do you do, Miss Caldicott?"

"Rested, thank you," she replied with a slight, repressive nod. She did not wish to encourage a flirt, not in the circumstances. Not in any circumstances.

He was as beautiful as she remembered, with rich brown hair brushed forward in a Brutus. His coat was somber enough for the occasion, also brown, with dull buttons that Clio supposed his valet had sat up late to change. His cravat was immaculate, a modest work of art.

In contrast, Mark, who appeared to be in his middle teens, wore a shabby riding coat over a drab tunic. His hair was uncombed, his complexion muddy . . . and his mother unheeding.

At the end of the room an elderly butler was placing a selection of viands on a dish. Because his hands trembled slightly, he was slow and careful. When all was to his satisfaction, he handed the plate to the footman whom Clio recognized from last night. He, in turn, placed it before her and inquired if she desired coffee or tea.

She chose coffee, and it was poured.

There was no conversation. All attended to their

plates, except Halloran, who stared with some pleasure at Clio. He would not have been true to his own nature if he had not noticed an enticing lady, even though his attentions made her uneasy.

What Clio did not realize was that, facing the long windows of the room as she was, the morning light caught her golden hair. The sun was on the other side of the house, of course, yet the illumination was strong here. The white ruffle at her throat framed her face sweetly. To anyone interested, as Hal was, she looked fresh and delectable. Not like a companion or a village maid or a West End Comet or a take-in, but like an unspoiled young lady whose pretty face and quiet manner were quite refreshing.

Presently Mr. Hampden set down his cup, remarking that he would go "to the bank." He, like Hal Linville, was tall. However, he had undistinguished features. Graying, clear-eyed, with thoughtful brow, he gave the impression of competence. Whatever his business with a bank might be, Clio felt instinctively it would be handled sensibly and well.

Eleanor watched his progress through the drawing room. When he had disappeared into the foyer, she addressed Clio in her colorless voice: "I have a number of matters calling me, you understand. You might like to stroll around the lawn until I am free. Someone—perhaps you, Hal?—will get the London stage schedule. We will provide your fare, of course."

"I have money," Clio said, embarrassed.

"I say, Eleanor," interrupted Halloran. "There will be people coming and going, notes to write, and all that sort of thing. You have no secretary. I daresay Miss Caldicott would not mind being useful for a time."

Eleanor looked surprised but was prompt to agree. "I do not wish to see people today. Would you stay, my dear?"

Avoiding Hal's eye, Clio signified she was willing to be of service.

"Thank you," said Eleanor. "Take a walk in the fresh air. I will send for you when I need you."

Then both she and Hal laid aside their serviettes and departed.

Mark continued to chew.

"Shall you mind being left alone?" Clio asked politely.

He cast her a surly glance and made a growling noise which might equally have been yes or no.

Avoiding eye contact, Clio had been looking out the windows at the lawn where Teddy was running and brandishing a stick. At this moment she saw him trip, tumble, and begin to howl.

"He may be hurt!" she cried, jumping to her feet.

The dud across the table volunteered three words: "Has a nurse."

"Oh!" she exclaimed indignantly. "No one is coming. He is still crying." Casting Mark a fulminating glare, she flew through the service door and down the steps. Soon she could be seen, if anyone had looked, pelting across the turf toward the child. Before she had reached him her slippers were soaked from the dewy grass, and by the time she had knelt and enfolded the boy her skirts were surely sopping.

"What is it, dear? Are you hurt?"

In a masterpiece of contortion Teddy managed to hold out an arm while burrowing into her embrace and continuing to cry lustily. To her relief she saw a simple scratch about two inches long and oozing only a bit of blood.

"Why, it's the merest scratch," she said.

The yelps increased dramatically.

"I think you are only bamming me," she added sternly. "You wretched boy! Trying to trick me because I am a stranger."

Though the child's bellows continued, they were in decreasing decibels.

"Sit up," she commanded, "and look me in the eye, you rogue."

There was sudden silence. Then she caught him peeking at her with a grin. "Aha! I shall immediately summon a dragon to deal with you unless you tell me what this is all about."

"But I was *hunting* a dragon," he declared. "His claw scratched my arm dreadfully."

She asked, "Were you expecting Maybelle to come?"

"No. She's feeding Baby."

"Your mother?"

"She's gone somewhere."

"Then who?"

He ducked his head and wiggled. "Wel-l-l, Uncle Hal—or you, maybe."

Clio gave him a rocking hug. "You got me, and I got you. We will now march to the kitchen for hot water to wash that mortal wound."

Teddy chortled and rolled away happily in the wet grass before scrambling upright. Then he came and held out his hand as if he were large enough to help her rise. She accepted the warm little paw and staggered to her feet.

As they walked toward the kitchen door at the end of the house, Clio shook out her damp skirts and thought how long it had been since she had actually *played*.

In the kitchen Cook took charge and cleansed the wound, clucking how sad it was that his grandmother would not be there to take him to the new toy store in Wendel as she had planned.

"Should his mama see this scratch, Cook?" Clio asked.

"Gone," said Teddy unemotionally. "Papa will make it well."

"Is he at your house?"

"No. Studio, I 'spect."

"Loft, miss," interpreted Cook. "Over the carriage house."

Teddy said, "I'll show you," and took her hand to lead her out the door. "Papa paints wunnerful pictures."

"Wait, miss," said Cook. "The sun's not warm yet. You will be cold in that damp frock. Here. Take a shawl." She seized a shawl, one of several articles hanging near the outside door.

"You may be right," Clio admitted. "Thank you." She tossed the garment about her shoulders and knotted it at her chest. Teddy reached for her hand again. "This way."

Their route led along a pebbled path through a kitchen garden where vegetables struggled to outdo each other in their race to extinction at the dinner table. At the carriage house an open stair ran up the near end to a yellow door in the gable.

Pulling away, Teddy plowed up the steps shouting gleefully, "Papa, Papa. I have a wound! *Mortal* wound, Papa!"

The door opened as he approached the top, and Clio, coming more slowly, was glad to see the boy warmly embraced. Roland Linville, eldest of Lady Linville's offspring, was a modified version of Halloran— a little less tall, but not short, eyes a cooler green, hair brown but less curly. His manner also was less flamboyant—and considerably more sensitive.

"You must be Miss Caldicott," he said, helping her up the final step and drawing her inside.

Here light was as clear and bright as outdoors, for panes of glass had been let into the slanting roof.

"See, Papa, I was clawed by a dragon," said Teddy, demanding immediate attention.

"Hmm," said Roland, as he examined the extended arm. "I did not think we had any dragons in the neighborhood. Not for the last several hundred years, anyway." He and Clio exchanged smiles. "You had a narrow escape, son. I see the uh—wound is minor."

"Does it need medicine? Or a bandage?" asked Clio. "I thought you should be the one to decide."

"No," said Roland, "but I believe a medal would be in order for this combat service." He produced a coin and bestowed it on the small hero, who shouted joyfully and ran off with his treasure. "I'm saving for an elephant . . . and I need more of these," he called back.

Roland followed to the top of the steps. "But not from wounds!" When he returned to Clio they smiled like old friends, perfectly at ease with each other.

"Now, don't you go yet," Roland said. "I come up here to be alone, but—somehow—today I feel lonely."

"If you wish." She looked about for a place to sit and then promptly forgot about doing so. The whitewashed loft was splashed with colors. Paintings, landscapes, of all sizes and shapes hung everywhere. Clio gazed at them with her lips parted in fascination.

"Teddy said they were wonderful," she managed finally.

"What do you think?"

"I? Why, I think they are splendid. Simply splendid! I can hardly leave one to go on to the next." Indeed, her progress down the room was slow. "Have you sold many?"

"No. I—well, I've never tried to sell."

"Why not?"

Roland, who had begun to expand, looked uncomfortable. "Helen thinks it's nonsense. How do I know they are worth anything?"

"Worth anything! Why that water is *wet*—and that bark is *rough*—and look at this one: these leaves are *blowing!* Doesn't anyone take these seriously?"

"Mother liked them—but of course she would, being the artist's parent."

"Poppycock!" exploded Clio, echoing one of her papa's expletives for which she was immediately ashamed, though Roland did not seem to take offense. She continued more moderately: "There are extremely handsome paintings in your mother's house. She ought to have recognized talent. Well, admittedly, I am no authority. You should show some to a dealer."

"Helen would have a spasm."

"Would she if they were worth money?"

Roland was silent.

"Would she?"

"Helen respects money," he allowed. "See here. You must not hold wrong ideas about Helen. . . . Try this stool. . . . She's not unfeeling, just very—well, practical." He paced a restless circle. "The trouble is the demmed bank."

"What bank?" asked Clio, perching on the stool.

"My father's bank in Scudderfield. A puddle of a town, but the only bank easily accessible to this side of the county. Let me explain. The Hall, the manor, the title were all entailed upon my elder half brother, which galls Helen, though it is an inescapable fact. And he has two sons. Malcolm is a fine chap. A true brother. I admire him excessively.

"Father, being fond of all of us, and having accumulated some of his income, established a small bank—not entailed, you see. He employed the younger son of a friend—who needed an occupation as I did—to set the bank on its feet. Edward Hampden. The best possible choice! Under him the bank has thrived, until we have recently launched

another in the market town of Wendel. Father kept
the presidency for himself, but Edward had free rein.
He has the incredible sense to know to whom he can
lend money, and to whom not—has the unique way
of saying 'no' to folk and making them his friends. I
came into the office when I finished at Oxford. Edward, by Father's will, is Chief Officer and I am just
about anything. Helen is dreadfully jealous of
Eleanor's husband, yet wishes I were more like him.
She thinks every minute I am up here I *ought* to be
adding interests."

Clio said, "A dead end?"

Roland smiled ruefully. "You know how it is. Most
every child has some ambition. Mine has always been
to paint—you see I haven't outgrown it. Eleanor used
to talk about being a missionary—can you believe it?
As for Halloran, he escaped Papa's design . . . goes off
to dig up ruins in some odd place of the world or
another. Sees himself as another Elgin, one supposes.
Helen—Helen likes to—rule. Good Lord! The sym-
phonic action she nurses out of half a dozen commit-
tees! There! I can see you are trying not to smile. It is
all right. Go ahead."

Clio threw back her head and laughed, nearly toppling from the stool. "You talk with all the color of
your paint pots," she declared. "All families are a little
mad. Well, Mr. Linville, I can be more practical than
your wife. If you feel compelled to paint, make it pay!
My father always told his students to work toward a
goal. Over and over he told them."

"Thank you. You are a very understanding young
lady."

"Papa had a friend who knows a great deal about
art," she added. "Mr. John White Rawl, in Bedford
Square. If you write to him, I feel sure he will come
and give you an appraisal." She extended her hand.
"Good-bye. Good fortune."

Instead of returning to the house via the kitchen garden, as Teddy had brought her, she followed the carriage drive around concealing shrubbery to reach the gravel space at the front door of the house. In daylight, now, she could see that the entrance drive had come up in a three-quarter circle to the top of a cliff. Hence the house faced almost due east. The rectangular central block and end wings were of mellow brick with cut-stone trim. The main part seemed oldest. Whoever had made the additions had skillfully matched styles. The whole effect was charming.

Apparently the family regarded it as a small home, but to Clio it was spacious. Eleanor had said the right wing held the library, with Lady Linville's apartments above it. To the left was the kitchen wing, the kitchen itself being set lower in the ground to provide the ventilation of a high ceiling. Her own chamber was above this, facing west. She knew, from having rescued Teddy there, that a wide lawn separated the house from the cliff's edge. The view must be glorious, though she had not had time to notice it.

While she was admiring the graceful urn that stood within the broken pediment above the main entrance, Halloran Linville came riding from the stables on a gray and white horse. She observed that he sat with the casual ease and perfect style of a nonesuch. His face had been browned by a sun of warmer climes. While it was not the color of an English face, it was pleasing to look upon.

"Hullo, hullo, Lady Helper," he said jovially. "Pray do not think this poor animal is mine. It belongs to my ham-handed nephew who runs the poor creature into the ground in an effort—which seems demented—to undo all its schooling."

"I am the last one to know the good points or bad points of a horse," she replied frankly, "but I would like to know why you are riding it if it is such a sad specimen."

"Ah! You are using your pretty head." His eyes swept her from top to toe, obviously considering more than her head.

The horse, perhaps exhausted by Mark, pointed one hoof like a ballerina and hung its head. Hal swung to the ground, retaining his hold of the reins. "It is my good deed of the day, to ride Charger. I put him through restrained paces and cultivate his manners. Say 'good day' to the lady, Charger."

Charger said nothing.

"You see. Already he is learning to be discreet."

It was impossible to snub such a convivial gentleman, even though Clio realized his soulful gaze was a sham. "I do not think you can teach him much in one day," she averred primly.

He was the picture of innocence. "Dear lady, I work him every day. A great deal can be accomplished in a short time if a gent puts his mind to it!"

Was he speaking of horses or gullible young ladies?

"Oh, yes," he went on, "today I will get the London stage schedule, but there is no hurry about *that*. There is one thing more important that I must ask you."

"Yes, Mr. Linville?"

"Are you any connection to Mr. Samuel Caldicott whom I heard lecture gloriously about Greek settlements in Asia Minor when I was at Oxford?"

Clio glowed. "Indeed yes. He was my father. He was invited to speak there several times and at Cambridge, also."

"Then I have *another* reason for being glad to meet you," Hal said with the flattering attention of which he was fully capable. "I always regretted he was not a permanent professor at Oxford. Will you believe that Mr. Caldicott's seminars had a profound influence on my enthusiasm for ancient cultures?"

She could believe it. "You might have guessed the relation on account of my name."

"Your given name? But I don't know it."

"Clio," she confessed, blushing.

"Ah, yes. Clio. The muse of History. Where is your laurel wreath? And your box of parchment rolls?"

To be flattered by an expert is enjoyable, yet it can catch one's breath. She was momentarily speechless, though being intelligent, she had begun to doubt his sincerity.

"That blue ribbon will do as well as laurel," he assured her. Being a master at dalliance, he gave her a saucy grin, mounted, and sent Charger down the driveway at a gallop.

For a few minutes Clio was so mesmerized that she did not see Helen approaching from a path to the Linville cottage. They were only a few steps apart before Clio saw Roland's wife. She had begun a shy smile, when Helen said bitingly: "How dare you! It was bad enough to come here unwanted—uninvited. Have you no shame? No, none! Why are you still here when we do not want you?"

Clio stuttered, "Mrs. Hamp—"

"It is some filthy scheme," Helen declared. "Encroaching! Hurtful! But this is worse—to dare take Lady Linville's shawl."

The shocked and confused girl raised a shaking hand to the knotted fabric on her bosom. "This?"

Helen was storming, not listening. "You have no right. Take it off. Take it off at once!"

With trembling fingers Clio untied the shawl and Helen snatched it from her. "You must go away!" she commanded harshly. Then she spun and ran away down the path.

Neither Papa, nor Papa's friends, nor Mrs. Mellow had ever spoken to her like this. White and shaken, Clio fled into the house.

Five

Mercifully, the door opened easily. Clio toppled inside, closed the door, and sagged against it. Her heart raced and thumped, although whether from fear or anger she did not know. It was an experience she had never had before.

Breathing rapidly, she drew herself up and prepared to fly up the staircase to her room. At that moment, midway of the flight, she discovered an apparition, a pallid woman with hair nearly white and trailing black garments.

For an awful moment, her senses being scattered, she supposed the creature to be Lady Linville.

"I'm—" she began, but could not continue.

The phantom's eyes were dark, very dark, not like Eleanor's or Roland's or Hal's. Her *stillness* was absolute.

While Clio stared, the white face suddenly crumpled into a million pieces, like a shattered mirror. To meet this strange creature—to pass on the stair—was beyond Clio. With a gasp the startled girl darted into the drawing room and raced via dining room, pantry, and service stair to the sanctuary of her chamber. She shut the door and threw herself to her knees against the bed.

"Lord, why am I here?" she whispered aloud. Was she being punished for coming into this grieving family? For acting rashly—without Mrs. Mellow's advice or

permission? Her aloneness seemed immense and end-
less. Even without Helen's caustic words Clio knew she
was not wanted here. What help could she possibly
be? She did not understand these people. Why did
Roland shut himself away from his family? Why was
Eleanor so frozen? Why was Hal so flippant with his
mother dead and not yet buried? Why was Helen so
hostile? The servants and a little boy showed more
sorrow than Lady Linville's children!

As these thoughts went through her head, she became more calm and was able to scramble to her feet
when Eleanor tapped and entered.

"Miss Caldicott!" Eleanor said in a concerned
voice. "What has happened?"

Trying to smile, Clio admitted that she had been
frightened. "I thought—I seemed to see a ghost upon
the stair. You will think me very silly," she rushed on,
"but I was—troubled—when I entered, and then I saw
a strange, silent figure—"

"You saw Plummy. Janet Plumb. My mother's devoted maid, whom we children always called
'Plummy.' It was she, you know, who insisted that I
come and comfort you."

"It *was?*"

"Yes. She thought Hal might have upset you. She
had seen him from an upper window before she
started down. Was it Hal, dear?"

"Oh, no," Clio blurted, "it was—"

"Helen?"

Clio compressed her lips.

"So it was!" Eleanor sighed. Her face was frozen,
as it had been all along, yet her voice was kind. "I
hope you will be forgiving of our humors, Miss Caldicott. We are not ourselves at this time."

She said nothing directly relating to Helen, so Clio
apologetically mentioned that Mrs. Linville had been
very angry to see her in Lady Linville's shawl.

"My mother's shawl?" She sounded more puzzled than annoyed.

"It was hanging in the kitchen with some other things. I did not know whose it was. Cook gave it to me to use," Clio explained.

Eleanor said, "Oh, *that* shawl. If Cook offered it to you, you can be sure that it was proper for you to accept. I have worn it myself from time to time."

Bent on setting matters straight, Clio repeated that Helen had been very angry.

"Mrs. Linville is emotional," Eleanor replied with the calm of one who was *not*. "Do not let it trouble you. Now, my dear, messengers and callers are beginning to arrive. You can help me greatly by meeting them, keeping lists, and so forth. There will be food and flowers to receive. I simply cannot face anyone today." As Clio nodded, she continued, "You will find writing materials in the office under the stairs. Can you manage? The servants will be there to assist, but callers will expect more than servants. Better change your dress, dear. Let me unfasten the buttons."

To Clio's astonishment, Eleanor went away without showing any curiosity about how Clio's dress had been wetted, soiled, and mussed.

This time, choosing from the few remaining items of her wardrobe, Clio was obliged to select a sprigged muslin. It was somewhat lower of neckline, but with buttons down the front which meant she could dress alone without ringing for a maid.

She descended to the main floor, and as no visitors were present or knocking she went on a quick tour. The Gold Parlor, across from the drawing room, was very handsome with gold satin hangings and a gold-veined marble mantel. Here, in a wide, ornate gold frame, was the portrait of a lady. Her eyes were looking directly at the viewer. The eyes as well as the nose and mouth were very much the same as Eleanor's, although there was a hint of humor and personality that Eleanor did not have. Lady Linville, of course, was the source of Halloran's vivacity.

From the Gold Parlor she went down three steps into a beautiful library which had windows facing both east and west. It was a darkly paneled room, though not dark itself because of six tall windows. Instead of bookcases along the walls, there were shelves cunningly built into the deep recesses of the windows. On the east side there were cushioned window seats in the alcoves.

Before she could examine the books for familiar friends, thuds of the knocker at the front entrance signaled the arrival of visitors. Clio hastened up and across the Gold Parlor.

A footman was just admitting a middle-aged couple. The lady was encased in black taffeta and the man carried an ancient black hat. Both wore troubled expressions.

"You are so kind to come," she said. "Mrs. Hampden is resting just now and the gentlemen are away. I am Miss Caldicott."

Having never heard of Miss Caldicott, they looked at her in some surprise, and being reassured by her excellent manners and ladylike appearance, launched into tangled condolences.

"We came as soon as we heard—" began the gentleman, at the same time his wife was saying, "Such a kind lady." And he finished up, "—the news." He clicked his tongue. "Never any problem with that cliff that I can remember."

Clio dealt with them graciously, being careful to ask their name.

"Mr. and Mrs. Wellenmanger," the woman said, "from Rose Cottage."

He spelled it carefully, and Clio repeated it punctiliously.

When the callers had gone, she hurried to find what Eleanor had labeled "the office." The central hall of the dower house, she now found, ran through to the west front and a terrace, although it was narrower at the back, having been partitioned for a cloakroom. To the left, opposite the cloakroom, was a door to the dining room which she had not previously noticed. Under the stairway, between it and the cloakroom, was a smaller hall with a convenience stair at the end. From here a door took her to an ample, if lesser, room facing west. It was the one she sought.

A desk between the windows offered assorted writing materials. Clio took two sheets, writing upon one the names of the first visitors. After a moment's thought she added the approximate time. Then, taking the second sheet, she crossed to the dining salon and from there to the service pantry.

Buckets of flowers waited here. The footman was in the act of separating perishable foods from ones which would not rapidly spoil.

Clio began to jot a list of items, matching them carefully to cards and notes. She had not half finished when two women came up from the kitchen. Middle-aged, they wore similar blue dresses and unbleached aprons. She supposed them to be servants from the Hall, but they identified themselves as tenants' wives, meaning to take endangered meats and puddings to cold cellars. She scribbled as fast as she could and succeeded in slowing the women only because of their awe of the strange young lady who was so pretty, so competent, so courteous to *them,* and so unknown in Scudderfield. What they would have to tell when they reached home! Dower house servants could have explained matters, but loyally remained mum.

She was so busy that she did not notice some dishes were advancing to the dining salon. Others arrived to take their places, having been handed in at the kitchen door. One tottery woman came herself to the pantry to say tearfully, "Lady Linville always admired my raisin scones, so I've brought some."

Clio thanked her warmly, sad to think Lady Linville would not enjoy these.

From time to time her list-making was interrupted by trips to the drawing room to greet new visitors.

One, in a rusty black bonnet, said sincerely, "We will miss her ladyship's book reviews at the Thursday Club."

A plump young woman lamented, "The one thing my grandma looked forward to was her ladyship's visits."

The nebulous figure of Lady Linville began to emerge as loved, loving, and wonderfully approachable.

Clio was just preparing to do something with the flowers when the butler came to announce that luncheon was served. The morning had flown.

Lunch was a matter of family members straggling in, by one and two, to munch at the groaning table. Clearly no one had an appetite. Eleanor remained above-stairs, but descended near the end of the meal to consult her brothers.

"There are people we must notify—Malcolm first of all," she reminded.

"I sent off a courier to him first thing. I do not know if he can reach home in time for the funeral," her husband said.

"There will be others. Mama's brother in Bristol. And Lady Cora."

Halloran, who had been lunching primarily on a series of cups of tea, set down his cup with a crash. "Good God! Lady Cora!" he shouted.

"No profanity, please, Hal," said his sister. "Of course we must notify Lady Cora. She was Mama's goddaughter."

"She may be here sooner than you think," he replied ruefully. "I saw her at the house party at Sanbourne's—"

"And you had the nerve to invite her for a visit!"

"Not at all. She invited herself. Said she wanted to see Mama. Dare anyone say 'no' to Lady Cora?"

Clio listened with cocked ears. What sort of person was Lady Cora? What age? What temperament? She heard Mr. Hampden ask when the lady was apt to appear.

Halloran shrugged. "There's no knowing. She was on her way to Bath and would come here afterward. Oh, what a lark she will make of this!"

"Lady Cora is not so as unfeeling as that," Eleanor corrected firmly. "She was truly devoted to Mama."

"Well, yes," he agreed. "But there will be no heading her off. I do not know where to reach her."

Eleanor pushed back her chair. "Let us go into the office and make a list. Come along, Miss Caldicott. We'll need you. Have you finished in the pantry?"

"The food, ma'am, but not the flowers," Clio answered.

"The flowers can wait," Eleanor decided. "They are in water, are they not?"

Until then Helen had sat wrapped in black clouds of general disapproval, ignoring Clio. She muttered, "I have letters of my own to write," and walked away toward the front of the house.

The remaining five went across the hall to the office.

Eleanor motioned Clio to sit at the desk, and the others distributed themselves around the room. "Before we make lists, let us consider this matter of Lady Cora. You know we have no room for her here."

"Billet her at The Hall," Halloran advised.

"Certainly not. There is no hostess there to receive her."

"True," said Mr. Hampden in a tone of no-non-sense which settled that matter.

Clio began to say, "Perhaps I—"

"No," interrupted Eleanor. "We are responsible for you."

Hal snorted. "Besides I cannot imagine Lady Cora in a room over the kitchen."

This time his sister pursed her lips forbiddingly. "Nor can I. She will have *your* chamber and *you* will remove yourself to the Hall."

Obviously this did not please Hal, although he stretched lazily and drawled, "Almost out of danger."

It made Lady Cora sound predatory.

Clio's curiosity quadrupled.

"If Lady Cora does come, we will all know how to behave, I think," Eleanor responded. "Now, let us put our minds to a list."

It did not take long. The uncle in Bristol. Some cousins in London. Another in Paris. Certain friends around the county.

Clio made notations.

"A simple message will do for all. Clio can write them for us and we will sign. Most by you, Roland, as head of the family—"

"Excluding Malcolm, naturally," Hal said, with a twist to his mouth. Did he dislike his half-brother? Roland had said they were all very fond of him, Clio remembered.

"Sir Malcolm may be anywhere," Mr. Hampden pointed out. "The notes must go out today."

"Any plan will suit me," Hal said, lolling back in his wing chair. He seemed in a strange mood. "Just write, 'We regret to inform you that Lady Linville died as the result of an accident Friday evening. The funeral is yet to be arranged. Yours faithfully. Etc. Etc.' "

"Very well," consented Eleanor, "only let it begin, 'We are distressed to inform you . . .' "

"That will serve," Roland said gruffly.

Mr. Hampden nodded.

With a heaviness that seemed more mental than bodily, Eleanor rose. "While Miss Caldicott is preparing notes for us I shall return to my room." This the men accepted gravely.

Clio was left alone with fine quality letter paper and her choice of pens. She began to write diligently in her best, unembellished style, and after finishing the first note, held it up to scrutinize for errors.

Two simple sentences.

So little to write about a lady universally admired, but emotional language might have been—well, tasteless. She certainly did not mind preparing the notes, although it seemed to her that the Linvilles might have penned their own letters.

But then, they were branches of a noble line and handled things differently from what had been her experience.

She continued to prepare notes, while from time to time she could hear the knocker of the front door and the muted exchange of voices. When she had finished her assignment, rather than going to the drawing room herself, she boldly pulled the bell cord near the door.

A maid came promptly, the older one.

"I have written notes at the request of the family," she explained, gesturing to the desktop. "Will you be so kind as to tell Mr.—" Which gentleman? Mr. Hampden, she supposed, because he was senior in this house. "Mr. Hampden," she finished.

"Yes, miss," replied the woman. The puffiness of crying had gone from her face now. She was pale and composed.

Clio thanked her. By slipping up the nearby convenience stair, along the upper hall, and down the service stair, she was able to reach the pantry unseen.

There she began to divide the waiting flowers into vases.

It was true, she thought. Flowers did speak. Sometimes of good wishes—other times of love—still others of comfort, concern, and regret, as they did now. Almost like people, they were tall, short, slim and spikey, full-blown, bright, pale, languishing, clustered or boldly solitary. And all, like people, would ultimately fade.

She had not seen Teddy or Mark since early morning. The boy was obviously in the care of Maybelle. Mark, on the other hand, had taken his surliness off somewhere. Good riddance. She wondered that Mr. Hampden put no end to such behavior.

Eventually the flow of callers dried up, Eleanor reappeared, and all but Helen gathered in the dining salon for a high tea. To culinary gifts was added a full-bodied soup. Mark turned up, showing no real animation except when his mother hovered over him with second helpings. No wonder he had bulges that were strange for his age.

While they were eating with not much appetite, a note was handed in for Mr. Hampden.

"Excuse me, my dear," he said to Eleanor in his temperate way as he opened the missive. He scanned it quickly, explaining: "They have released Lady Linville's body for burial. Shall we proceed without Sir Malcolm?"

"I think so," she replied. "Roland? Halloran?"

"Tomorrow is Sunday," Roland reminded.

"Then it will have to be Monday. Afternoon, I believe. Will you speak to the vicar?"

"Yes. But morning might suit Helen better. She will want to take Teddy and Susan—and they have sleepy time after their lunch."

Eleanor looked distressed. "Oh, surely not the little ones! It will upset them. Why, I had not considered taking Mark." She slued her eyes to her son, who glowered at being discussed.

"You may do as you please with your offspring," declared Roland with unusual firmness. "Helen and I will decide for ours. Lady Linville was their grandmother, after all."

Eleanor led Clio away to the terrace while the men had their port. None of them wanted it, yet old habits die hard, so they permitted the ancient butler to pour each a few ounces to swallow without tasting. Mark, being too young for the trauma of his grandmother's funeral, was old enough for port. He tossed his off before shambling out to the stables.

After this gesture to convention, Roland, Hal, and Mr. Hampden followed the ladies to the west front.

On the apron of stone flags that fanned into the west lawn were set iron chairs of some comfort. Clio felt strongly that her presence was undesired and may have been resented. She took a seat at a distance from the family, wondering nervously if her returning inside would equally give offense. Was it her duty to remain available?

Artful planting at the cliff's edge prevented anyone who was seated from seeing the river valley. Tops of the hills beyond were just barely visible in the fading light. As she watched gold crests melt to silver and finally disappear in smoky shadows, Clio shivered a little. For the time being, the men in their somber coats were warm, and Eleanor held a light woolen scarf about her shoulders. She, Clio, would have to trot upstairs soon for a wrap if she did not want to freeze.

No one seemed to notice when she slipped into the house.

Although she saw lamps lighted in both Mr. and Mrs. Hampden's rooms as she passed, her own room was dark when she reached it. One window was open and voices floated in from the terrace. She groped for a tinder box.

"—must keep Mark out of it," said an anxious voice below.

"Shush," cautioned another.

"She went inside. She cannot hear anything." That was Mr. Hampden's deep voice.

"Upstairs windows are open," said another.

Clio carefully set down the tinder box and stood, arrested, in the darkness.

"There is no light in her room. She cannot hear."

Hear what?

The rest of the words were indistinguishable.

Somewhat shaken, wildly curious, and slightly nervous, Clio tiptoed down to the library and took up a magazine as a sort of alibi.

Presently, Halloran stuck his head in the room. "Oh, there you are. I wondered what had become of you."

"I thought I would read a little," Clio said, trying to seem natural.

"Out of *Baily's Racing Register?*"

Having not read a line of what she held, she said quickly, "Why not? Did you never look at *La Belle Assemblée?*"

"Good Lord, no!"

"You should. It might help you to understand women."

"Oh, I understand wo—" He began to laugh. "Well, maybe I don't, at that!" He shook his head and continued to the main stair. She heard his footfalls on the treads.

He did not remember to ask if she had been in the library all along.

A little shaken because he had nearly exposed her as a liar, Clio released a pent breath. She followed across the Gold salon, and when, halfway to the staircase, she heard a door latch overhead, she ran lightly up the flight and across the transverse corridor to her room. A moment later the butler passed down to fasten locks and extinguish lights. There were faint sounds of Mr. and Mrs. Hampden coming to their rooms. Doors closed.

Had Roland walked across the dark lawn and woods to reach his cottage? It must be a perilous path, unless he had the eyes of an owl.

As for herself, she closed her window and was soon jumping into bed to think.

There were a great many questions that needed answers, chiefly concerning Lady Linville. Was her death an accident, or not? How odd that the family said nothing one way or the other! They made no speculations. Showed no worry about details. No searching for reasons. No anger, only regret. The fact, Clio thought, of the family's being so unquestioning about the death might indicate that all of them supposed only an accident had occurred. It was simply an unfortunate death.

And here I am in the midst of it all, she said to herself. *You would think they would resent me, but they don't.* Except, of course, Helen, whom Clio considered to be quite mad.

Was anyone investigating? Would they ever *know*?

When one is young, healthy, and tired, and tucked into a cosy bed, it is very difficult to stay awake.

Six

Sunday dawned clear and sweet. Gentle breezes had carried off the mistiness of the day before, and the hills across the river were plainly visible from Clio's room. When she opened her window to breathe the freshness of the morning, she could actually see a house and outbuildings on the opposite slope.

Clio missed the noise and bustle of London yet found this rural tranquility wonderfully soothing.

Sunday, in London, had always been a day for Clio and her papa to dress in their best and go to St. Giles for worship. Even when she was a small girl, her papa took her to that church with its burial plot rising around it, expecting her to absorb the atmosphere even if she did not understand the words. He often said the knowledge of classical antiquities, which he enjoyed, had taught him to appreciate the wisdom of the Bible. He and Mr. Lambton were quite in accord on *that*.

Mrs. Mellow had also been in accord—at least, in the matter of church attendance. In nearly two years she and Clio had not missed a service.

But here, at an hour when she and Papa would have been sharing breakfast, no one stirred. She dressed in the sprig muslin frock again and went softly down the service stair to peep into the dining salon. There were five places set, all untouched, and an array of covered dishes on the sideboard. There was no sign of servants.

She retraced her steps to the pantry and descended to the kitchen where she discovered Cook dozing in a chair by the fire.

"La, miss!" exclaimed Cook, rousing with a start. "Would you be looking for something to eat? It is ready—in the dining salon—unless you would be wanting something else."

"No, no," Clio replied hurriedly. "Everything looked delicious." If one could see through silver lids . . .

"You must help yourself, miss. Mr. Hampden has already had his."

Clio mentioned that she had not seen a used place, and Cook replied that she dared say Mr. Hood or Fralke had re-set.

"Mr. Hampden has gone off to take Plumb to the Hall. She would not rest 'til she saw milady laid out proper. Trusted no one else to do it, though there's ones at the Hall that loved her, too." A long sniff followed this.

"I wish I had known her. Everyone seems to have been so devoted," Clio said sincerely.

"Aye," agreed Cook. "A grand lady as ever was. It seems fittin' for her to lay in the chapel up there. It was her home a long time."

Clio asked if the funeral would be conducted at the chapel.

"Oh, no, miss. Not enough room. I think they plan some sort of service—"

"Memorial?"

"Aye. At the church in the village. So everyone can come, you see. Then a burial next to her husband on the hill. Two services, you might say."

"I see," said Clio.

She returned to the dining salon and ate a hearty

breakfast. Afterward she went about checking water in the many vases she had arranged the afternoon before. Mr. Hampden did not return. Nothing was heard from other members of the family.

Bells sounded faintly from Scudderfield.

Apparently no carriage would be going to the church.

She ran upstairs to fetch a shawl, then went out by the front door for a walk. Since the last thing she wanted to do was encounter Helen Linville, she turned in the direction of the carriage house and stable.

Doors stood open at the carriage house, and she saw an ancient though well-preserved black chaise and a tilbury. Wheel marks showed where a smaller vehicle—perhaps a dog cart?—had been drawn out. There was no reason for Lady Linville to maintain a large fleet when all the equipment of the Hall was available to her.

Stable doors were open wide, but no horses showed their noses.

Coming upon a path into the woods, Clio ventured on it, pleased to enjoy an experience she did not have in London. It made her think of Wordsworth's *Descriptive Sketches*.

Where the path branched she saw that the left branch disappeared downhill, which meant that she would have to climb back again, so she turned right. This path meandered with gentle rises and falls until presently trees thinned out and she emerged to the crest of the cliff where a wide stone wall defined a sort of lookout.

"Visiting the scene?" asked a young man perched there.

"Oh," said Clio, surprised. "Is this where—but she could not have fallen. Not with this wall."

"I wonder," he answered obtusely, rising to his feet

politely, if not the better to look down at her. He was a head taller. "Who are you?"

He was hatless, brown hair combed back casually from his brow. His well-cut riding coat, though unembellished, sat smoothly on wide shoulders. The coat was dark, serviceable green. She thought he might have introduced himself more properly. There was nothing menacing about him, so she gave her name: "Miss Caldicott."

"What are you doing here?" He spoke mildly, yet was firm enough to require an explicit answer.

"Does it matter?" she retorted shortly. "This is private property. What are *you* doing here?"

"The same as you. Visiting the scene."

Clio said impatiently, "But I am not . . . just who are you?"

"Hugh Stamford. Representing the magistrate of the district."

"I see. The—"

"Ogre?"

Clio smiled faintly. "You should know. Shall you be pestering these unhappy people?"

His expression did not change. Watching her with lustrous brown eyes, he motioned her to sit upon the wall, which she found herself doing. "Why are you here, Miss Caldicott?" He seated himself nearby. "I mean, what is your business at Savaron Hall?"

She considered the toes of her slippers. "I am—well—you might say, Lady Linville's companion."

He looked surprised. "Companion? At the dower house? Does anyone know about it?"

The wall was at least two feet wide, and she felt secure enough. Looking past Mr. Stamford, who was on her right, she had a glimpse of Scudderfield downstream, lazy in the morning sunlight. She could see the bridge across the river and the weathered roof of

Mr. Brill's inn. It was a beautiful spot—where Lady Linville had fallen.

"Everyone at the dower house knows."

"First I've heard."

"Do you mean no one has mentioned me?" she asked, incredulous. "Less than a nuisance, then. A nonentity!"

"No saying what is on their minds," he reminded solemnly.

"You are right. I was not thinking. To lose a dear one is very . . ."

He nodded and stuck a dead pipe in his mouth.

"I do not mind if you smoke," Clio offered. "My papa cherished his pipe."

It was his turn to show a slight smile. He said, "No tobacco."

By leaning carefully on her right arm Clio could see the road below where Lady Linville had met her death.

"How far is it?" she asked.

"Down?"

"Yes."

"Sixty feet or so. A good jump."

"Lady Linville did not jump."

He looked at her closely. "Why do you say that?"

"Because Teddy said—"

"Teddy! Was he here? Did he see her fall?"

She had his instant attention. This was another new experience, for she was accustomed to her father's friends who patted her on the head, talked to Papa, and ignored her. She was, after all, a mere female. Mrs. Mellow had added to the lesson by giving her kindly hints that young ladies had nothing to say which would interest the superior intellects of gentlemen. They, she had explained, expected eager *ears*—and pretty, ladylike manners.

"He was not here," she replied. "That is, I do not

think he could have been. He is heartbroken, but has
no frightening memories."

"So what did Teddy say that matters in the least?"

"Enough to show that she did not jump."

"How can he know? Do you credit a child's prattle?"

A smile teased the corners of Clio's lips. "See here!
I have a real respect for Teddy's opinion. If you must
know, she promised to take him to a new toy shop in
Wendel next week."

He adjusted his pipe. "And that was supposed to
keep her from jumping? A child begging for a treat?"

"Ah!" cried Clio. "That is just it. He did not beg.
She offered! *Cook told me.* Besides, there's me."

Mr. Stamford continued to look thoughtfully at her
face. He asked, "What about you?"

"Mrs. Linville wrote without telling anyone. I was
to come because she had need of a companion."

"With so many in the house?" he suggested doubtfully.

She admitted they seemed surprised to see her.
"Would she have asked me, if she had been thinking
of jumping?"

Mr. Stamford removed the empty pipe from his
mouth, tapped it unnecessarily against the wall. Instead of answering her question, he inquired mildly
when she had come.

"Friday evening," she said. "If you had talked to
Barney Brill he would have told you. He plucked me
from the stage."

"Like a flower?" he teased unexpectedly.

"No. Like seaweed left on a beach. Wilted and
damp. The Linvilles weren't happy to see me, I fear,
but were too kind to cast me out in the night."

The pipe returned to his mouth, and he sat thinking
deeply.

Clio waited. She had little to tell. Perhaps he would

tell *her* something. The Linvilles certainly had not
done so.

"You did say Friday evening, didn't you?" he asked
finally. "There may be something in this. What time
would you say?"

"Between eight and nine, I suppose."

"Mrs. Linville was dead."

"Yes. The stage was two hours late. She was dead by
the time I reached here. Mr. Brill brought me from
the inn. You can ask him. I came on the stage from
London just as Lady Linville suggested in her letter."

"What letter?"

"The one to Mrs. Mellow—my employer. She asked
me to come as her companion, and it sounded—"

"I would like to see that letter," he interrupted.

"Well, you cannot. It's gone with Mrs. Mellow to
York. You can write to her, but very likely you won't
believe her any more than you believe me!" Clio's
voice quivered with indignation. "There certainly was
a letter."

Showing he was not unreasonable, he said: "All
right. So there was. I would like to see who wrote it."

"Who wrote it! It was signed 'Mary Linville.'
Couldn't she have done so?"

"Unless someone signed her name." He pursed his
lips as if determined not to believe her.

"Why would anyone do that? Good gracious! There
is nothing mysterious about hiring a companion."
Truly, he was as impossible as he was handsome.

He retorted, "There is an inescapable fact that you
arrived for some unsubstantiated reason at a time
when a rich woman fell, jumped, or was pushed to her
death. Good day, Miss Caldicott." He strode off in the
direction from which she had come, both he and she
wondering if he could suspect her of a crime.

"Merciful heaven!" breathed Clio, gaping after him
in dismay. She looked again at the low, wide wall,

moved from it, and shuddered. The day which had
seemed so splendid became forbidding. She was loath
to imagine Lady Linville's death as anything but acci-
dental, especially since each hour was adding some
favorable detail to her picture of the old lady.

Who could want to kill her? The Linville children
seemed stunned. The servants, if Cook were any example, were shattered. Villagers had rallied round
with condolences which were obviously genuine.

"Blast that man!" she muttered to herself, continuing on her way to the house. "I believe he said that to
torment me."

Maybe she believed it and maybe she did not. At
any rate, the dower house had become downright sinister when Clio came through a clump of lilac bushes
and found herself on the green acre of lawn. There
was the same stillness as the night of her arrival. Mul-
lioned windows reflected daylight with a vacantness
that said *gone. Gone.*

Overcome with loneliness, she entered the main
hall from the terrace and roamed stately rooms, hungry for human contact. Through a front window she
could see the dog cart waiting emptily, which meant
Mr. Hampden had returned, with or without Janet
Plumb. Would the woman have finished preparing
Lady Linville? Clio had not seen her since that odd
sight on the stair.

In the pantry she met Molly, the redhead, who was
descending the steps with a load of clothes.

"Don' know top from bottom," the girl complained, "what with Miss Eleanor and Miss Helen both
givin' orders. Look at all these clothes! And Mr. Hal
askin' for shirts. I don' know who wants what."

"They probably do not know either, Molly," said
Clio. "Everyone is rather mixed up. Was this supposed
to be your free day?"

"Only afternoon, miss."

"I am sure Mrs. Hampden is grateful for the way you have stayed to help things run smoothly."

"Ta, miss," Molly said, appeased. Her dimpled arms moved swiftly as she rolled and dampened garments.

The kitchen, down eight steps, was large and obsolete, which did not matter to Cook as she herself was dated and would not have known a patent range from a washing dolly. Cook was in her proper sphere. She was baking something spicy now. It teased Clio's nose. Clio knew luncheon would be succulent, for Cook was creating meals with the obvious conviction that rich food was balm to grieving hearts.

Presently, voices sounded in the front part of the house. Clio hurried to the hall, where she found the household gathering. Even Mark, still groggy from a late morning in bed, was present as they drifted into the drawing room to await Mr. Hood's summons to the table.

"Have you any duties for me, Mrs. Hampden?" Clio asked.

"No," said Eleanor vaguely. "Unless—the flowers may want water. Oh, have you already seen to them? That is all for now, I think."

"Good," said Halloran. "Miss Caldicott has seen nothing of Savaron Hall. After luncheon I shall drive her around the manor."

No polite invitation for her to go.

"You will enjoy a drive on such a fine day," he informed her. "Just within our land, Eleanor. There can be no objection."

Eleanor made a small gesture with her hands. No contest.

"Perfect weather," Halloran declared. "You won't need a bonnet, Miss Caldicott. We'll stay off public roads. . . . I say, Hood, the dog cart is still out front. We won't want that. Tell them to switch it for Pensive and the tilbury."

The butler inclined his head an inch and snapped two fingers, dispatching the footman at once, which surprised Clio greatly. No one else appeared to take any interest in the matter.

Not a little miffed, Clio briefly considered declining the invitation which had not been issued. Then she remembered that she had seen nothing of the baronet's manor and house. She might never visit a country estate again. It was a rare opportunity.

She bestowed a long, thoughtful glance upon Hal, who chuckled. "You need a treat," he told her blandly.

For other unacknowledged reasons she politely and softly yielded with thanks.

After the meal Hal took her arm and led her to the gravel space where the forty-year-old footman, Fralke, came driving up quickly in Lady Linville's tilbury. Apparently, the man could do double-duty as groom, for he immediately sprang down to hold the horse. Triple-duty, Clio thought, if he had harnessed the animal himself.

Halloran helped Clio climb to a seat in the vehicle.

"Pensive is as ill-named as Charger," he said, taking his own place beside her. "Never will travel as slow as a walk!" He gathered the reins, and the footman stepped back. They were off at a fast trot.

"My mother," Hal said, "did not believe in wasting time. On the other hand, she claimed she was too old for galloping horses. Pensive has been schooled to trot indefinitely."

Down the driveway they rolled, catching a glimpse of Roland's cottage amidst trees to the left before they turned right toward the Hall.

For at least twenty minutes—perhaps thirty—they sped along well-kept lanes, seeming to take left or right branches at random.

"Are you sure we have stayed within the manor?"

she asked. They had met no traffic, yet had covered a lot of ground.

"I am sure," he responded. "I want to watch what crops have been put in. See what pruning might be needed. Malcolm has an excellent bailiff, you know— my father trained him. And I do not interfere, but I like to—well, reassure myself. Malcolm owns it. I love it."

She could detect no resentment in his tone.

"I'm the youngest in the family," he continued. "I had no expectations. You might think Roland, as my mother's eldest son, would have his nose out of joint, but he doesn't. Malcolm was only four when my mother married my father. Malcolm instantly became her son. We never were a family without him as our elder brother. Besides, Malcolm is the best of fellows."

A little stream tumbled along beside the road now, and they followed it to its source, which was a wee lake girt with rocks artistically arranged.

"Isn't it beautiful?" Halloran demanded.

"Charming," she replied.

"I mean the whole manor," he said.

"Grander than Hyde Park," she avowed.

He laughed. "How cosmopolitan you are!"

Pensive trotted untiringly along, while Hal explained that the main entrance to the manor was eastward from Scudderfield. "This way you will see meadows, crops, woodlands—everything."

And she did, breathless with the loveliness, awed by the perfection with which all was maintained.

When, at last, he pulled Pensive to a halt under the shade of a great oak tree, she leaned forward in astonishment.

"Behold the Hall. Not big, but beautiful," he said.

To her eyes it was huge, truly not as large as Hampton Court or Windsor, yet sprawling generously, mostly two stories and in some parts only one. Clio, the classicist's daughter, was stunned by a conglomeration of Tudor wings, Queen Anne, and Georgian—the result of Linville whims over generations.

"You are speechless," Hal said, pleased, as he switched reins to one hand.

She turned back to him, only to be seized by a free arm and soundly kissed.

Miss Clio Caldicott had never been kissed by a man before this. She found it a curious sensation—neither pleasant nor unpleasant. Not at all what she had imagined from reading the thrilling novels that Mrs. Mellow borrowed occasionally from Hookam's Library.

"Well, well," said Hal softly. "Very sweet and ladylike. You can do better than that!" He lowered his head again, but she recoiled, pressing a hand against his chest.

"Little prude!"

"No, sir, a big one."

He laughed lightly and set Pensive in motion.

Up to Savaron Hall they went, traveling twice along the front. The stone core, he explained, had been an abbey. "Norman, I think. It is very old. You can count periods. Not much in the classical line, which is my field, but I love it all."

Clio's ruffled feathers and flush had begun to subside. She asked with effort at composure, "Then why do you go off to the South—and Asia—for such long stays?"

"I have to make a life for myself," he replied flatly. "As youngest son, I gave some thought to the opportunities of India, but my mother forbade it. Diseases there, you know."

"I would not suppose bans would stop you," she said with a sideways peek.

"True. Love of Mama did."

She liked the sound of that, and began to forgive his behavior to herself.

"Do you wish to see the inside?"

"Yes, but no," Clio answered. "You must realize it would not be proper."

"Not for Miss Proper Caldicott," Hal said with a cheerful grin. He turned the tilbury and on the return journey talked so casually and agreeably that they reached the dower house on tolerably good terms.

Seven

Fralke admitted them in his usual role of footman. Mr. and Mrs. Hampden were in the office and wished to see them, he said.

"Right," said Halloran. He motioned Clio to go before him.

When they entered, Mr. Hampden looked up and seemed glad of reinforcements. Eleanor's face was wan.

"My courier has returned from London," Mr. Hampden said heavily. "He saw only Malcolm's secretary, as Malcolm and young Lady Linville had gone to Essex for a visit to her parents. The secretary promised to send off a message at once, but he felt there was little hope Sir Malcolm could come anytime soon for a funeral. It seems our little lady is threatened with miscarriage, and of course he cannot bring himself to leave her."

"They are so devoted," murmured Eleanor forlornly.

Her husband bracingly replied, "We may count *that* as a blessing, may we not?"

She nodded, but lamented that her brother would be so distressed to miss his mother's burial.

"He will have the felicity to remember only the happiest and fondest of memories," Hal pointed out.

Clio, standing ill at ease at this emotional moment, wondered if Hal's own memories were equally affec-

tionate, and immediately had her question answered
when Hal, with a catch in his throat, added, "—as our
memories are."

Eleanor buried her face in her hands, though not,
as it turned out, to weep, but to pull herself together.
"Well, then. We must manage without Malcolm. We
could never wish him to desert the dear girl. Miss
Caldicott, an immense quantity of flowers has come
from General and Mrs. Stamford. Will you be so kind
as to arrange them for me? You do it beautifully."

"Certainly, ma'am. In the pantry?"

"Yes, dear."

Thankful to be released from the tensions of the
office, Clio slipped quietly from the room, although
the names General and Mrs. Stamford echoed loudly
in her head. She heard the men begin to discuss plans
for the next morning as she went.

"Immense" was no exaggeration. Buckets of
blooms, mostly exotic orchids, had come from the
Stamford glass-houses and thirstily awaited attention.
Clio reveled in them; she had never before handled
orchids. She spoke to them in an undertone. "Hold
your head up!" "Slip in here." "Yes, you can." "Stiff-
en your spine, please." She created a dramatic dis-
play for the long table in the hallway. Having placed
it there, she returned to make a lesser cluster for the
office, the only room on the main floor to which she
had not carried vases.

The door to the office had remained open, so she
entered with the vase, saying into a lull, "Shall you
want these here, Mrs. Hampden?"

So obviously was the girl a lady, so pretty with a green
ribbon catching back her curls, her manner so naturally sweet, that the two men unconsciously sat
straighter, and Eleanor actually produced a smile as
she said, "How lovely. Yes, put them on the desk. It
was generous of the Stamfords to send them."

"Yes, yes," allowed Halloran somewhat impatiently, "but why must we tolerate Hugh's nosing into our affairs?"

Mr. Hampden answered calmly, though his expression was severe, "We have an unexplained death here. The truth must be discovered if we are to have any peace of mind."

"Mrs. Stamford wrote a charming note to me, explaining why they could not come to us at this time. The general, poor man, is housebound with a broken leg," added Eleanor, forgetting for a moment her own troubles.

Clio heard all this with astonishment. So Hugh Stamford was a gentleman of some standing! Well, she had thought his appearance pleasing, if not as stunning as Hal's, and his manner of listening to a lady courteous . . . until he had become cross at her and stalked off. Was he hoping for a crime to solve and notoriety to win?

Eleanor and Halloran had fallen into a squabble about the Stamfords' Whig bias versus the Linvilles' temperate Toryism, when Hood came to say there were callers approaching the house.

"Oh, dear," said Eleanor regretfully. "They are kind to come. I suppose I must see them. Edward? Hal? Join me."

Not feeling needed in the drawing room, Clio seated herself at the desk to add the Stamford name to her list of flowers and food received. It could not be supposed that the family actually required either. Not food, with all the resources of a manor at their command, and servants to prepare it. Nor flowers, as she had herself seen extensive gardens during her drive with Halloran. It was a way for friends and neighbors to show their concern. Even the small offerings of villagers were warmly acknowledged by Clio. "How kind—so lovely—"

After a time, Halloran returned and sat in a nearby chair to ask about the list and correct her spellings of some names. His place in the drawing room had been taken by Helen, who had come up from her cottage to discover who was at the dower house and to be greeted as a Linville, Hal said.

Helen soon tired of this, since there were no visitors of significant stature to hold her interest. When Roland appeared to augment Eleanor and Mr. Hampden, she wandered down the hall in search of Hal, who was usually more amusing, and entered the office in time to see Hal laughing easily at some joke of his own, and Clio smiling with a pen slack in her hand.

"Miss Caldicott!" cried Helen. "You were not hired to dally with gentlemen!"

The object of the attack stared at her in shock. Clio was not of an irascible nature, but did have limits of tolerance. She said decisively, "I have not been employed and I am not being paid."

Hal turned bright red. "Good God, Helen!" he burst out. "Just let Eleanor hear you say that!"

"I *have* heard it," said Eleanor's voice from the doorway. "Miss Caldicott is my guest. You will apologize immediately, Helen."

"When you have apologized for misleading me!" retorted Helen. She pushed past Eleanor and they heard her staccato footsteps in the hall. The front door slammed.

Eleanor said sadly, "Only Mama could keep Helen in her place."

"And Mama could do it gently, too," Hal amended. "We are desperately sorry, Miss Caldicott."

"I understand," answered Clio, trembling a little with shock.

"We are truly grateful for your help," added

Eleanor to Hal's apology. "I did, indeed, mean to repay you."

Clio averred that she was glad to be useful somewhere and would begin writing notes of thanks if Mrs. Hampden wished.

The knocker sounded.

"More callers," moaned Eleanor, "and Edward is all by himself—"

Somewhat sheepishly, Halloran followed her down the hall. And presently Roland, who had encountered clouds of fury at home from his wife, walked in to see what had happened. Until the callers all were gone, no explanation was forthcoming, but when the last had left, Eleanor and Hal unburdened themselves quite frankly.

"Helen has some frightful moods," Roland admitted. "Shall I ask pardon of Miss Caldicott?"

"No," decided his sister. "Miss Caldicott would surely prefer to forget the whole scene."

And Hal agreed.

"The worst part is," lamented Eleanor, "I need to ask more of her."

Hal said, "May be the best cure."

"What do you mean?"

"That you *are* grateful and *do* need her."

"Inspired!" said Roland.

And Mr. Hampden added in his sensible way, "We are most fortunate to have Miss Caldicott here, and not some half-bred female all too ready to take offense."

By Sunday evening the household had settled into its accustomed pace. Family and servants went about their usual activities. Appetites had revived enough to do justice to the full dinner which Cook thought they needed after emotional famine.

"How many carriages will we want in the morning?" asked Mr. Hampden, the practical one.

A round table discussion settled on four: Roland, Helen, and their two oldest children in Roland's chaise; Eleanor, Edward, Halloran, and Plummy in Lady Linville's black carriage; and two others from the Hall for servants of long standing, of which two were Mr. Hood and Cook.

Both Mr. Hampden and Hal made some effort to dissuade Eleanor from exposing her grief to public scrutiny at the church, but she insisted it was her wish to attend the memorial and hear what the dear vicar had to say about her mother.

No mention was made of Mark.

If he bestirred himself to go after all, Clio imagined they would pack him in somewhere. What, she wondered, was he so sulky about?

She did not fail to notice that no provision had been made for herself. At this time Eleanor suggested diffidently that since Miss Caldicott had never known Lady Linville, there was no reason for her to go with them. She probably had no mourning clothes or black gloves, did she?

Clio nodded yes, no reason, and no, no weeds. It was a scrambled response which Eleanor took to mean as suited her.

"There is one thing, though," said Eleanor with a conscious lowering of her eyes. "I am ashamed to ask more of you, but would you—would you keep yourself available in case Lady Cora should arrive while we are away? She would expect someone other than servants to welcome her."

Hal made a strangled sound, as if burying a laugh. "Lady Cora would make mincemeat of our Miss Caldicott."

"Not at all," Mr. Hampden contradicted in his assured way, and his wife shot him a grateful look.

"I am glad to help in any way," Clio said firmly.

"Thank you, dear," said Eleanor. "You won't have

to stay in the house every minute. The maids and the houseman will be here, if only you will tell them where to find you if you wish to walk outside." She hesitated apologetically. "After the church service we will be going to the Hall for the burial. Mr. Linville's room will be prepared for Lady Cora. Will you see that she is served tea if she comes while we are gone?"

Clio and Hal spoke at once, Clio saying "Certainly, ma'am," while Hal suggested, "Suppose she goes first to the Hall?"

Mr. Hampden's deep voice said reasonably, "She won't do that if she is expecting to visit your mother."

Though Mr. Hampden looked somewhat stodgy, due to thickness in the midriff and an indifferently tied cravat, Clio was beginning to realize that his mind went immediately to the essence of any matter under discussion. Since the family was dispersing with no claims on her time, she chose a book from the library and went to her room to read a while before settling to sleep. Mostly, her mind puzzled over the Linvilles, so that she actually read very little that night.

At breakfast on Monday all were subdued, talking little. One by one, family members drifted from the room. As maids came in to clear the table, Clio took a last sip of coffee and went for a quick circuit of the public rooms to be sure the flowers were all fresh. The best place for herself, she decided, was the office, where she could keep busy writing notes for Eleanor to sign. That way, she would be out of sight, yet available. Assembling for the carriages, they would not want strangers around. She knew from experience how tense those last moments could be.

The front door was standing open. She could hear the crunch of wheels upon the gravel. There were footsteps on the stairs, and a murmur of controlled voices. Then all faded away. The door closed. She heard the measured tread of the footman walking to his seat in the back of the hall.

Two years since Papa . . .

She put her hands to her mouth and squeezed her eyes tightly. *One never forgets, never,* she thought. *And one never wants to do so.* Pushing back her chair, she rose, laid aside the pen, placed a crystal weight upon the papers, and went into the hall to address the footman. How boring his duty must be!

"Mrs. Hampden must rely upon you greatly," she said to the man.

His face remained solemn but his glazed eyes brightened. "I hope so, miss," was his answer.

"Mrs. Hampden told me there is a possibility that Lady Cora may arrive to visit. Will someone please summon me at once if she does so? I will cross the lawn and enter the path at the lilac bushes. That is the shortest route to the overlook, I think."

He nodded a balding head. "Yes, miss. It is. I will come myself at the first sign of a carriage."

He opened the terrace door for her and she strolled slowly down to the terrace and lawn, finding refreshment and solace in the casual planting of trees and shrubs, the pale clear blue of cloudless skies, and a feeling of infinity in the rolling hills across the river.

When Halloran had taken her to view the Hall, its immensity and incongruity had so overwhelmed her that she had completely failed to notice the Hall's own outward view in any direction. She had not thought it could be so lovely as this. Perhaps this was one reason Lady Linville so readily relinquished her former home to Sir Malcolm and his wife.

She said softly to herself, "This is difficult to resist."

As she rambled down the path a faint, sweetish aroma reached her nose and grew more pronounced as she advanced. Clio well knew the odor of tobacco and hoped she could guess its source.

Today Mr. Stamford rose to greet her. He wore a blue coat, more sharply tailored than his green, yet moderate in style. By this time he knew certain things about her, and she about him, which caused him to be more cordial and her more diffident.

"I thought you might come," he said, implying that he had hoped she would.

"Why? I might have gone to the church service or—"

"Or taken a walk to escape the oppression of the dower house?"

Liking this more amiable side of his nature, she smiled at that and sat upon the wall. "Not oppression exactly. Really just an atmosphere of sadness. I thought this beautiful day and place would give me a new spirit."

"A common virtue of nature!"

"Yes. Not a new idea, I suppose," she admitted. He looked calm, composed, neat, gentlemanly, not hostile at all, so she said, "But you do not need the assistance of nature."

"Not today, at any rate," he said. "I hoped to see you free of the Linvilles, for I have something to tell you." He sat beside her and idly emptied the pipe. "I talked to Brill and he verified your coming on the late stage."

"So. You did not believe me!"

"I did not disbelieve or believe," he answered placidly. "Father expects me to bring him facts, not beliefs. Now, how can I verify that you boarded at London?"

Indignation driving away her hesitant manner, she said crossly, "By the waybill. Or by writing Mrs. Mellow. Or if those won't suffice, you can write Mr. Thatch who set me upon the stage at London. I have never met with such distrust in my life!"

"Yes, but you have never been involved with an unexplained death, have you?" he replied mildly. "Father may want to talk to you himself. You would not mind? He is a great gent."

"More than that, I expect."

"Yes, more. Not intimidating, but inquisitive by nature and takes his office seriously."

Clio yielded with a nod. "A magistrate should."

"Very well, then. While he is housebound with his leg propped on a stool and can soak up attention from my mother, tell *me* what you know."

Clio said she knew almost nothing.

"Then begin with the household. Who is there now?"

She ticked them off on her fingers. "Well . . . Mr. and Mrs. Hampden, Mark, Mr. Halloran Linville, the butler, a footman, two housemaids, Cook, and Lady Linville's maid—"

"Plumb?"

"Yes. I have not seen any valets and should think a nonesuch like Mr. Hal would have one. Maybe Mr. Hampden also."

"They may have kept out of sight, in their masters' rooms, or ones of their own in the attic."

"I suppose that is possible. I've seen Plummy only once." She did not admit to thinking Plumb was a ghost. "The upstairs maid may do for Mrs. Hampden. You would think she would have a dresser."

Mr. Stamford remarked that the Linvilles took great pride in their family but cared little for high fashion. "I cannot think servants have any motive for—uh—crime. What would it profit them?"

"They seem genuinely crushed by the death of the old lady," Clio said.

"Old lady!" exclaimed Mr. Stamford. "She wasn't old at all. Fifty-four, I would guess. My mother is in her fifties and I can tell you she doesn't consider herself ready for a Bath chair!" He stared thoughtfully at his empty clay pipe, tested it for heat, and stuck it in a pocket. "It seems Lady Linville fell while the family, including Teddy, was at dinner?"

"Yes. I saw the disrupted table."

"Who was actually there?"

"I don't know. Hood would be the one to say. I saw the table and it was set for eight. Two places were not used."

"One was meant for Lady Linville?"

"Yes. But something was said about her asking for a tray in her room."

"Only she wasn't in her room? Obviously not. Well, who else was missing?"

Clio hesitated. "I think—perhaps—Mark."

"Mark? Why Mark?"

She answered slowly, "Something was said—I heard—oh, I cannot like to call names."

"I can ask them," Mr. Stamford reminded. "It would be better for you to tell me."

Clio bit her lip. "This makes me feel like a traitor. They are all so kind—*except* Helen. I just can't—"

"See here, my girl," said Mr. Stamford, sitting up straighter. "Where are your loyalties? To Lady Linville, I should think!"

She sat frowning at her own thoughts. "I wonder if anything I could say would matter. I'm here by accident, you might think. I don't know these people—or their hopes and fears. It would be *treacherous* of me to expose their—emotions!"

"But I am not asking about emotions. This place must be seething with those. Just tell me what you heard and let my father figure it out. No one in this household is going to be at peace without an answer to Lady Linville's unexpected death."

"All right," Clio submitted with a sigh. "I heard someone—do not ask who because I don't know—say, 'must keep Mark out of this.'"

Mr. Stamford pursed his lips thoughtfully. Even like

that he had a nice, well-balanced face; his eyes were contemplative. "Out of what? Maybe I can discover that without disturbing any of the family. Can you tell me anything else?"

She shook her head.

"It may be that all seems perplexing when it is only very simple. I mean, we might be looking too deep."

Clio said she hoped so.

"Will you keep your eyes and ears open for me?" he asked.

"Like a spy?"

"No. Like one who desires justice. If someone killed Lady Linville, he must pay for it."

Clio asked, "Suppose it causes more pain?"

"Murder," he retorted, "is *never* justified."

There came a sound of running feet. Both sprang up. Clio started toward the path through the bushes. When she glanced back at Mr. Stamford he had disappeared.

"Oh, miss," panted the footman, coming into view, "Lady Cora's chaise will have reached the house."

"Then let us make haste," she responded and gathered her skirt to scurry to meet the lady. The footman, who had longer legs, was able to slow his speed and still keep pace with her.

In the hall two anxious maids were receiving a dazzling creature with red-gold hair cascading from a high-poke bonnet of emerald green. Her traveling cloak of emerald velvet fell from one shoulder to reveal a gold frock of simple though striking cut. Her face was flawless ivory, finely sculptured.

Clio had never seen anyone so beautiful. Faithful to her instructions to provide a welcome, she went forward and said, "Lady Cora! I am happy to welcome you. The family is away just at the moment, but should return soon. I am Clio Caldicott."

The glorious being surveyed her with a glance that

swept from head to toe. There was no haughtiness in her bearing. Evidently satisfied that Miss Caldicott, an unknown, was no servant, she extended her hand, and Clio stepped forward to take it tepidly. A maidservant, who stood a step behind her mistress, Clio acknowledged with a civil nod.

The hall was becoming crowded with the two maids, Molly and Miller, Lady Cora and her attendant, Clio, and the footman who was helping Lady Cora's groom to stagger in with luggage.

"Do come into the Gold Parlor, Lady Cora, and we will have some tea," Clio urged.

"That will be just the thing. The last lane has juggled me into a pudding," replied her ladyship. "What room am I to have?"

"The east room. Molly, pray escort Lady Cora's maid there and see that she has some tea also. Miller, bring ours to the Gold Parlor as quickly as possible."

"I always thought the east bedchamber was Hal's," said the lady as she accompanied Clio into the parlor and dropped her cloak and bonnet casually on a chair before choosing a seat for herself. "He is not here now?"

Clio said, "At the Hall, Lady Cora. Mrs. Hampden wanted you near to her."

"I see. Keeping Hal at a distance from you." Lady Cora studied Clio's face. "I suppose it was Lady Linville's idea. Is he up to his usual tricks?"

"Pardon?" said Clio, endeavoring to subdue a blush.

Lady Cora's laugh tinkled. "He cannot resist a pretty face. Well, you may be easy. I shall take him in hand. Now tell me where everyone has gone. Surely he told you to expect me."

"Yes, but not when."

Miller brought the tea tray, and Clio was thankful to have a breathing space while she debated what to say next. When she had served Lady Cora and taken a cup to bolster herself, she said regretfully that she had bad news.

Lady Cora halted her cup before her lips. "I loathe bad news. Must you tell me?"

"I think you would prefer to hear this before the family returns. Lady Linville has died."

"Died! Why wasn't I informed?" The cup rattled as she set it in its saucer.

"They did not know where to reach you."

Lady Cora moaned, "Poor dear, dear Godmother! And I was only an hour away. Have I missed the funeral? Of course! That is why the family is away from the house now."

"They should be coming very soon," Clio said.

"What happened? Tell me all!" her ladyship commanded. She pursued facts much as Mr. Stamford had done and soon was saying vehemently that Godmother never, never would have killed herself.

"That doesn't seem likely," Clio agreed. "I understand that she was vigorous, busy, not old nor troubled."

"And such a darling, did you not think?"

Clio admitted, "I never knew her."

Lady Cora drew a handkerchief from her sleeve, wiped her eyes, and demanded, "Who are you?"

"Someone who came to be her companion. She wrote and asked me to do this, but she fell to her death Friday evening just before I arrived."

"Then you are not some trick of Hal's to put me off? Why, this is sad for you, too, although in a different way from us." The tears began to roll down her cheeks, the first adult tears Clio had seen shed for Lady Linville—other than by servants. She found Lady Cora rather overwhelming in person and vitality, but the grief seemed genuine. She waited, not knowing what to say and judging to say nothing was better than to offer sticky platitudes.

Presently, Lady Cora blew her nose delicately and observed that perhaps it was well she had had this private word with Miss Caldicott. "Am I to understand that there is some doubt the fall was an accident?"

"If you know the overlook—"

"Perfectly!"

"—it seems odd that she could have fallen."

Lady Cora fixed Clio with stern and intelligent eyes. She asked, "Has the constable looked into this?"

Clio answered that she believed he had been in touch with the magistrate.

"Oh, General Stamford. Excellent man. Has he been looking for facts?" Yes, thought Clio, Lady Cora was awake on all suits. She said Mr. Hugh Stamford was home on a visit to his parents and had been pressed into service by the general.

"Hugh? That's a mercy. *He* will get to the bottom of things. Very bright. Represents the neighborhood in Parliament, you know. I shall have to have a word with him."

"Parliament?" queried Clio, surprised.

"Yes. Younger son, but going far. Has gone, as a matter of fact. If Halloran would just get over this wanderlust of his! . . . I really think I must do something about Hal."

Wondering what Lady Cora might attempt, Clio said, "But he is very happy exploring—or whatever it is!"

Lady Cora dismissed this with a casual, "Oh, a lot of exotic nonsense."

At which Mr. Caldicott's daughter said, "I cannot think heat and dirt and strange food can be alluring."

"Of course it isn't. And it certainly is unnecessary for a Linville."

"But he *likes* it."

"Pooh!" retorted Lady Cora. "He likes fine clothes, doesn't he? And smart carriages? And sleek horses? I think my manor outside London would suit him very well. Convenient to the metropolis, you know, with dashes to Newmarket for the races and to the continent in slack seasons. A husband in the eastern Mediterranean would not suit *me.*"

Emboldened by this open talk from a stranger, Clio asked, "Are you betrothed, ma'am?"

"Not yet," replied her ladyship. "Godmother wished it, but I have not made up my mind. I can afford him, and he *is* charming. Do you not agree?"

Rather astonished by such frankness, Clio nodded. Her own notions of matrimony and romance were culled from fiction, Mrs. Mellow's gentle guidance, and the connubial harmony of Mr. and Mrs. Lambton, and were totally at odds with Lady Cora's.

"Females are forever swooning over Hal and pandering to his pride," Lady Cora told her. "I had supposed you were another in a long line."

"Oh, no!" protested Clio, mortified.

Lady Cora eyed her speculatively. "No? Well, perhaps not. You are very pretty, and I daresay Hal cannot resist trying his wiles on you?"

Clio gasped, "Yes—no!"

"Ah! So he has!" Lady Cora said with a small laugh. "Such a practiced flirt must find you a challenge. But do not be alarmed, for I am here to cope. Indeed, I must admit I would not find Hal so interesting if he were not an amiable devil."

To Clio it seemed a contradiction in terms, a devil being in her mind a personage waiting outside St. Giles Church to keep unwary folk from entering. She thought Halloran was amiable enough—that is, jolly—though kissing young ladies willy-nilly was really outrageous.

"Is the tea still hot?" asked Lady Cora, holding out her cup.

"I believe so," Clio answered. "Do you wish some?"

"Just a touch to warm what I have, please."

The two ladies were holding cup and pot when sounds of a carriage reached their ears. Cup and pot were hastily set down and the young women flew to a window.

They saw Halloran step first to the ground, then Mr. Hampden. Both reached into the chaise and extracted Plummy to place her carefully on her feet. As they turned back to Eleanor, Plummy hurried to the house with head bent. Miller held open the door.

Lady Cora, meanwhile, had sped into the hall where Clio's astonished eyes saw her fold the weeping servant into her arms. An earl's daughter embracing a maid! Clio understood at once that Lady Cora was a great lady indeed.

"I know. I know," whispered Lady Cora tenderly, quite undismayed that the old woman's tears were spotting her smart gold frock. "We loved her, didn't we?"

Eleanor, looking ashen in the face, entered leaning heavily upon her husband's arm. With no word to anyone they proceeded up the stairs. Lady Cora followed with Plummy.

Halloran was last to enter, and by this time Clio had drawn back out of his line of sight. She glimpsed Hood, also gray of visage, come from the back of the house via the dining room to say, "Would you wish anything, Mr. Hal?"

"Yes. Brandy. In the office, please."

Eight

The coming of Lady Cora, the Earl of Kelland's daughter, had a comforting effect on the residents of Savaron Manor, for her attitude to each was just as each unconsciously desired.

With the servants she was courteous, prefacing her requests with "please" and acknowledging every service with "thank you" and "oh, very good!" They basked in her approval and could not do enough to win it. To Eleanor she was kind and sustaining, to Helen solemnly respectful, to Halloran flirtatious. She asked Roland how his painting progressed and seemed able to converse on pigments and oils. Mr. Hampden was invited to explain the effect of parliamentary rulings on banking profits, which she pursued through a whole course at dinner.

When Roland whispered to Clio at dinner that Lady Cora seemed to understand one's problems, he unwittingly gave her a useful clue. He said that Lady Cora talked to each individual with focus on that person's particular concerns.

Sure enough, Lady Cora was soon observing, "You make your home in London, do you not, Miss Caldicott? Something interesting is always happening there, isn't it? I suppose the silence of the countryside keeps you awake here at night."

"It would," agreed Clio, "if the air were not soporific."

Lady Cora smiled appreciatively. "A clear conscience!"

"I'm afraid we wear her out," admitted Eleanor.

"But a clear conscience cannot be worn out," Lady Cora denied promptly. "Only muscles and nerves. Do you prefer the city, my dear?"

"I am obliged to, as I must live there."

"But you are living *here*," Halloran pointed out.

Helen snipped, "Writing notes is not arduous."

"No," agreed Lady Cora, fixing Helen with a frown, "not writing notes nor arranging flowers tastefully. Keeping one's temper is much more difficult for *some*."

Helen's eyes fell before Lady Cora's.

Clio thought guiltily that her own character must be flawed as she was glad to see Helen set down. She hoped no one could read her mind. Then, incredibly, Halloran winked and she knew he had done so.

"Did you close the bank today, Edward?" her ladyship continued calmly, addressing Mr. Hampden, and not disdaining commerce.

"Until three," he replied. "We wished to show all due respect to Lady Linville, but I felt depositors might suffer hardship without access to their funds. The bank was closed Saturday and Sunday also. I hope it was not unbecoming of me to oversee the clerks from three to five today."

"Not at all. You are not a Linville."

Helen looked as if she would like to complain, but Lady Cora continued smoothly, "Consideration for others is one of your nicest attributes, Edward."

An outspoken lady, Clio thought, who sounded older than her years! Perhaps it came of being an earl's daughter. Everyone seemed fond of her. One who was consistently *right* might irritate but never offend.

Hood and Fralke cleared away in their grandest style, with which Lady Cora found no fault, even if she very likely was used to having a footman stationed at her back for her exclusive service. A sweet was offered and then a savory.

Although Lady Cora's rank was highest, Eleanor, in the absence of her mother, presided as hostess. She indicated that the ladies would withdraw and led them from the room, Clio trailing.

The time had come, Clio thought, for her return to London, and if the Bath-to-London stage did not pass through Scudderfield too early on the morrow she must catch it. As the ladies strolled toward the library, she deflected toward the office, intending to lie in wait for Mr. Hampden whom she relied upon to send her to Mr. Brill. She only hoped the stage would not be crowded, forcing her to ride outside, which would be horrible, or wait over a day at the inn. To do that, without a maid to lend her consequence, would be humiliating, although Mrs. Brill might take care of her. How she wished for Mrs. Ames! What had begun in London as adventure had become terribly complicated.

Mark, as usual, had vanished by way of the kitchen, with who knew what intention? Mr. Hampden came from the hall door of the dining salon as she had hoped. She caught him under the stair, holding a paper and looking solemn. Roland and Hal were close behind him.

"Excuse me, sir," she said. "Obviously the time has come for me to return to London. The house is overcrowded and my usefulness finished. Can you set me on the London stage tomorrow?"

Eyebrows slanted in regret, and gesturing with the paper he held, Mr. Hampden said, "I am afraid not, Miss Caldicott. A note has just come from General Stamford asking that we make ourselves available to his son tomorrow. He specifically asks that you be present."

"Me?" cried Clio. "I know nothing about the accident!"

"Of course you don't. What questions the general may have we do not know. I can only suppose it is about Lady Linville's writing you to come. There will be other questions for us."

Clio turned doubtfully to Hal and then to Roland. Both nodded.

"We must do what we can to clear away all uncertainty," Roland said. "I expect the servants must be questioned, too."

"Yes, and I want to hear all the answers myself," Halloran declared.

"It will be a strain for Eleanor," Mr. Hampden said morosely. "Well, what must be, must be. We should set you on the stage the next morning for sure, Miss Caldicott."

Her situation was nowhere nearly so stressful as theirs, Clio realized. How could she object to mere inconvenience when they faced real grief? "Thank you, sir," she said to Mr. Hampden. "I will cooperate in any way I can."

Hal said, "Good girl. Now, Edward, let us break the unwelcome news to the ladies and hope no one has a spasm."

Clio thought, *Lady Cora won't.*

When the men had gone toward the library, she skittered up the little convenience stair to her room and to her speculations.

No sooner had she turned away from closing her door than her eyes fell upon her neatly turned down bed. The counterpane was laid back trimly, and lace-edged sheets were folded at an angle to invite her entry.

She gave a small gasp and whispered to herself, "The bed! I forgot to tell Mr. Stamford about the bed." She moved toward it and ran her fingers upon the pillow.

Had Lady Linville prepared the bed *herself*? Surely not. Molly would know, but how could she ask without raising unwanted interest?

Her gaze swept the room and hesitated upon the wardrobe where her few dresses waited limply.

Boldly she stepped to her bell pull and gave it a yank, hoping Molly would be the one to answer.

Molly it was.

"Oh, Molly, it was you, was it not, that restored my blue dress after my romp with Teddy?" Clio said. "Thank you so much."

Molly beamed and bobbed her head.

"The whole room is charming," Clio continued. "Did you choose the pretty bedding for me?"

"Yes, miss. Lady Linville said to use the best things for her guest and not to forget sachet."

Clio said, "Um-m-m delicious! I had sweet dreams all night because of it. So it was your choice! Thank you. If I wish to put on the blue tomorrow, can you help me with the buttons?"

"Oh, yes, miss. Certainly. Miss Eleanor won't want me before eight-thirty. Just you ring any time before that and I'll come. Mayhap you'd let me brush your hair, too. Miss Eleanor says I have a knack. I hope she will let me turn her out in fine style like the lady she is. She cares nothing for fashion—and her so handsome!"

"You would prefer to be a lady's maid?" probed Clio.

"Oh, yes, miss! Like Lady Cora's abigail . . . but there does not seem to be much hope."

Clio observed that it was always more convenient to be hopeful.

"If you say so, miss," Molly conceded doubtfully. She sketched a little curtsy and went away.

"I would like to do something for that girl," Clio said to herself as she undressed, "but what can I do?

I have no prospects of my own." Perhaps Lady Cora could suggest something for Molly, although Eleanor might think poorly of giving up a capable chambermaid.

In the morning her first thought was not for Molly, but for Mr. Stamford. She hoped he did not reveal their previous meetings. Eleanor and Lady Cora might be scandalized, and Helen was sure to be cutting.

She had worried for nothing.

Mr. Stamford arrived about eleven. He was received in the library by Mr. and Mrs. Hampden, Mr. and Mrs. Linville, Halloran, and Lady Cora, who had nothing to contribute, but was full of curiosity with Clio fading into the background.

It must have been uncomfortable for him to question the private affairs of longtime friends. Nevertheless, his manner was calm and tactful. He acknowledged the introduction of Miss Caldicott with a cool nod and began by asking, generally, if they had previously had any concern about Lady Linville's capabilities. A murmur of "no" rose from the circle of chairs. They were all in agreement about that.

"Now let me see," he said, drawing a small notebook from his pocket and a short pencil. "Did I understand the family was at dinner when the accident is presumed to have happened? Who exactly was present, Eleanor? You and—"

"My husband. Roland and Helen—oh, yes, and Teddy."

He jotted names in his book. "Halloran?"

"Yes."

"I believe the table was set for eight. Is that right? Who else?"

Eleanor bit her lip and said vaguely that her mother had not come down.

"Did you expect her?" he asked mildly.

"Well, I had done so, but Hood told me she had rung for a tray in her room."

Mr. Stamford made another note. "That makes . . . five, six, seven. Who else was present? Mark?"

There was a long pause. Then Eleanor unhappily said, "No."

Mr. Hampden shifted in his chair and offered, "Off on a lark of some sort."

"I wondered if he could be sleeping," Eleanor said. "The hours he keeps—"

"We really did not think about Mark," explained Mr. Hampden, seizing command of the conversation, "because Constable Tully came with the sad news and we went rushing out."

Mr. Stamford put away his little book. "And the young lady arrived while you were gone?" He glanced toward Clio, who nodded. "But unexpected?"

"That's correct," Eleanor confirmed.

"Well, I was expected by Lady Linville," Clio burst out. "No one believes she wrote inviting me, but Molly—the chambermaid—told me this morning that Lady Linville asked her to prepare my room for her guest."

The family stared at her in surprise.

"Easily verified," said Mr. Stamford calmly. "Miss—er—Caldicott was here when the family returned?"

Halloran told of finding Clio waiting. "She was not expected by *us*, but obviously we could not turn her off in the night."

"Certainly not!" declared Lady Cora.

"Miss Caldicott has been very helpful," Eleanor added.

"Fixing flowers," sneered Helen. "So important." Her husband looked at her reproachfully, which she ignored.

Mr. Stamford considered this with his tongue thrust into his cheek. He turned to Edward Hampden, inquiring if Lady Linville's doctor had been notified. "The local doctor says death resulted from the fall."

Lady Linville's personal physician was a sort of cousin who resided in Wendel. He was presently on a visit to the Lake District, Edward explained.

"I see. And her man of law?"

"Has his office in London. I have sent a message to him, asking him to come."

"Very wise," approved Mr. Stamford. "There could be something in her will to explain this mystery."

"Surely not!" objected Halloran.

"Probably not," Mr. Stamford corrected pacifically, "yet we do not wish to overlook anything that could be helpful. My father will have my head if I do not bring him all of the details, Hal."

Hal smiled at that and inquired about the general.

"Ready to call for the cannons," said Mr. Stamford, also grinning. "My mother is exerting all her small arms which are not, I promise you, ineffectual! I wonder—Eleanor, would you be willing to spare Miss Caldicott for a while this afternoon? Father is possessed to investigate the circumstances of Lady Linville's inviting her here, and Mama thinks a visit from a pretty young lady will do wonders for his morale."

He did not look at Clio when he said this, which was fortunate as her mouth gaped open.

Eleanor was equally surprised, yet uncritical. "Of course we can spare her to the dear general."

"May I call for you at three-thirty, Miss Caldicott?" he asked. "Do not be alarmed. This is no inquisition. My mother has suggested tea."

Embarrassed to be the center of attention, Clio mumbled something affirmative, and he turned back to Eleanor.

"Then that is all for now. If you have no objections, I will see the servants in the kitchen where they will feel more at ease."

"You know the way," Hal said.

Mr. Stamford bowed and left the room. They could hear his voice in the hall instructing Hood to summon the staff.

In the library all was quiet for a few moments.

Then Roland remarked that a friend in high places did make matters easier.

"It is only a ruse to catechize Miss Caldicott about our private affairs," Helen complained.

"About which she knows nothing," protested her husband, horrified at her gaucherie.

Clio had turned scarlet with embarrassment.

"Hugh Stamford is an excellent son. You may be sure he is thinking of his father's enjoyment," said Lady Cora firmly. "Halloran, let us take a walk. I need fresh air."

"At your command, my lady. I need fresh air, myself." He offered his arm and they exited by the front door.

Mr. Hampden fell into a low-voiced conversation with his wife, and Helen soon went away.

When Roland rose to follow her, he passed close to Clio, held a finger before his lips, and whispered, "I have written your Mr. Rawl. Do not tell!"

Her eyes sparkled. She compressed her mouth and ducked her head.

Roland departed, not ill-pleased.

"Come here, Miss Caldicott," instructed Mr. Hampden. "I hope you do not feel a martyr cast to Stamford lions? They are really kind people. The general inherited from his father soon after his own retirement from the army. An excellent man. And Mrs. Stamford is a baggage."

"Edward!" objected Eleanor, "you never describe ladies that way!"

"Well she is," he insisted stoutly. "You will see, Miss Caldicott. Go and have a carefree afternoon. I, for one, think we are fortunate to have General Stamford in charge. He will be more considerate than Bow Street."

Eleanor admitted that was true. "If you will dash off a note to Mrs. Stamford for the orchids, I will sign it," she said, "and let you deliver it for me."

The note was soon prepared, signed, and stowed in Clio's reticule. She decided to continue in the blue dress with which her plain bonnet would go nicely. The weather was balmy. Mrs. Mellow's cast-off shawl of thin white Scottish wool would be cover enough. She hoped she would not be maneuvered into telling anything detrimental to the Linville family, but as Mr. Stamford already knew as much as she, and probably a good deal more, that seemed unlikely to happen.

Halloran and Lady Cora returned in time for nuncheon, both with a high color, and Lady Cora with hair rather wind-blown. Clio wondered if he had kissed *her* under a great oak tree. She was a lovely lady by any standard, only two or three years older than Clio, though considerably more sophisticated. Her beauty and amiability, not to mention wealth, must attract many suitors. It was difficult to tell how serious about Hal she might be. The aggression was on her part, though he did seem to fall in line with whatever she wished. Of course, a true gentleman would be attentive to a guest in his home. It was a puzzle for which Clio found no answer.

After they had eaten, Lady Cora went to spend some time with Plummy, and such was the compatibility between the two, that they remained closeted in Lady Linville's suite for nearly two hours.

As Mr. Hampden was returning to the bank after the meal, Roland stopped in to ask if he were needed. "No, no, old fellow. No hurry. Come when you feel like facing people," his brother-in-law said. His manner was warm, though anyone knowing the family might think it did not matter if Roland ever came.

"Come talk with me, Miss Proper Caldicott," commanded Hal. He tucked Clio's hand into the crook of his arm and led her toward the library. There he seated her upon an Adams settee, taking his place beside her.

"Now, he said, "tell me what you think of Lady Cora."

Surprised at this directness, and wondering what value her opinion could have, she responded, "Splendid. A diamond of the first water."

"Very true," he agreed. "Yet I can remember her as a wayward brat who insisted on riding the most mettlesome horses in our stable—even if she frequently fell off. My mother was a girlhood friend of her mother. She visited us often."

"Was she always beautiful?"

"Yes. Always. That is, I suppose so. Her features have always been quite perfect, but what boy of ten or twelve—or even fourteen—takes notice of such things?"

"Her style is elegant, and she has a lively interest in everyone she meets," Clio contributed.

"Have you ever thought . . . that for a man to be serious about a lady, she must concentrate her interest in *him?*"

Clio remembered how Lady Cora had said, "I can afford him."

She mentioned hesitantly, "You saw how tender she was with Plummy." Wondering why she should promote Lady Cora's affairs, she added, "That indicates a warm heart, don't you think?"

He sprang up abruptly, saying, "Let us walk outside."

But Clio, having little understanding of her own worth, and full comprehension of her vulnerability, said hastily, "Not now. Mr. Stamford will be coming for me soon, and I must not keep his horses waiting."

We'd Like to Invite You to Subscribe to Zebra's Regency Romance Book Club and Give You a Gift of 4 Free Books as Your Introduction! (Worth $19.96!)

If you're a Regency lover, imagine the joy of getting 4 FREE Zebra Regency Romances and then the chance to have these lovely stories delivered to your home each month at the lowest prices available! Well, that's our offer to you and here's how you benefit by becoming a Zebra Home Subscription Service subscriber:

- **4 FREE** Introductory Regency Romances are delivered to your doorstep
- 4 BRAND NEW Regencies are then delivered each month (usually before they're available in bookstores)
- Subscribers save almost $4.00 every month
- Home delivery is always **FREE**
- You also receive a **FREE** monthly newsletter, *Zebra/ Pinnacle Romance News* which features author profiles, contests, subscriber benefits, book previews and more
- No risks or obligations...in other words you can cancel whenever you wish with no questions asked

Join the thousands of readers who enjoy the savings and convenience offered to Regency Romance subscribers. After your initial introductory shipment, you receive 4 brand-new Zebra Regency Romances each month to examine for 10 days. Then, if you decide to keep the books, you'll pay the preferred subscriber's price of just $4.00 per title. That's only $16.00 for all 4 books and there's never an extra charge for shipping and handling.

It's a no-lose proposition, so return the FREE BOOK CERTIFICATE today!

Say Yes to 4 Free Books!

Complete and return the order card to receive this $19.96 value, ABSOLUTELY FREE!

(If the certificate is missing below, write to:)
Zebra Home Subscription Service, Inc.,
120 Brighton Road, P.O. Box 5214, Clifton, New Jersey 07015-5214
or call TOLL-FREE 1-888-345-BOOK

Check out our website at www.kensingtonbooks.com.

FREE BOOK CERTIFICATE

YES! Please rush me 4 Zebra Regency Romances without cost or obligation. I understand that each month thereafter I will be able to preview 4 brand-new Regency Romances FREE for 10 days. Then, if I should decide to keep them, I will pay the money-saving preferred subscriber's price of just $16.00 for all 4...that's a savings of almost $4 off the publisher's price with no additional charge for shipping and handling. I may return any shipment within 10 days and owe nothing, and I may cancel this subscription at any time. My 4 FREE books will be mine to keep in any case.

Name _____

Address _____ Apt. _____

City _____ State_____ Zip _____

Telephone ( ) _____

Signature _____ RN1B9A
(If under 18, parent or guardian must sign.)

Terms and prices subject to change. Orders subject to acceptance by Zebra Home Subscription Service, Inc. Offer valid in U.S. only.

AFFIX
STAMP
HERE

ZEBRA HOME SUBSCRIPTION SERVICE, INC.

120 BRIGHTON ROAD

P.O. BOX 5214

CLIFTON, NEW JERSEY 07015-5214

"Damn his horses!" vociferated Hal, with laughter in his eyes.

"You may curse his team, if you please," she responded, moving toward the hall, "but I must cultivate his good opinion if I wish him to believe what I say!"

He commanded, "Wait!"

But she had already escaped up the stairs.

Nine

It seemed sensible, though cowardly, to wait in her room. Unfortunately, Clio could neither see the front driveway nor hear traffic upon it. She was obliged to depend upon a servant's notifying her when Mr. Stamford came.

The sun was now on the west side of the house. It shone upon her as she sat at a window dreaming a little, admiring the perfection of the lawn and shrubs. Evidently Lady Linville preferred vegetables to flowers, or else she was essentially practical about foods. Less cultivation of flowers could be found here than of vegetables beyond the kitchen. Did a gardener lurk somewhere? Surely Lady Linville had not grubbed in the beds herself! It might be that she had continued to give attention to flowers in the greenhouses near the Hall and did not need to do it here. But this was only speculation. The lawn *was* lovely, with dappled shade. Vistas one place or another drew one's eye toward the western hills. Nature was at peace, even if Savaron Manor was not.

Eleanor's, Mr. Hampden's, and Roland's temperaments coasted with the gentle currents of the countryside, she thought, while Helen and Halloran seemed to spin in multiple pursuits. Most restless of all was Mark. She wondered how he spent his days, amazed that a man so disciplined as his father could let the boy fritter away his time.

In the home where Clio had been reared there was
for many years a competent and beloved housekeeper
to see that all ran smoothly for Mr. Caldicott and his
motherless daughter. By the time the good woman was
too infirm for total responsibility, Clio had reached
fourteen and learned a great deal of household sci-
ence by a sort of domestic osmosis. It was a comfortable little family, augmented by the virtuosity of a
footman-valet. Also, they enjoyed the company of her
papa's friends. Mr. Caldicott was much admired in
scholarly strata. His friends coddled the pretty child,
bringing her sweets until she was old enough for
books. As she grew older, the tomes became both heav-
ier and weightier, yet she thanked the givers gracefully
and, for lack of other amusement, read all. Some she
thought hopelessly impractical, but she learned to understand the scholars' minds a good deal better than
did their own wives. *They* sometimes came for tea and
were delighted to help Clio with her needlework. Alas,
there were no children for her to romp with.

The Caldicotts had led a serene existence. Life was
conducted courteously. There was no occasion for tantrums by anyone or distress. The death of Papa was a
circumstance to be *met,* not railed against with angry
tears.

As the time neared three-thirty, Clio shook herself
from daydreams, brushed her blond locks, put on her
bonnet, and assembled her reticule and shawl.

Mr. Stamford arrived on the thirtieth minute.

His vehicle was a dark green curricle with cream
wheels, smart but not exotic. There was a groom in
dark green livery to hold the pair while Mr. Stamford
assisted her to her seat. When he had joined her and
taken the reins, the groom sprang to a perch at the
rear. Mr. Stamford signaled his black horses by some
minor motion of the lines, and the blacks responded
with scarcely a jerk to the riders.

Preferring to die rather than admit her nervousness in such a racy carriage, Clio observed politely, "Your mother was kind to suggest tea."

"She knows how to give Father pleasure," Mr. Stamford returned as a skillful compliment. "Is this not a beautiful day for a drive?"

Not wanting to take the general's pleasure to her own credit, she was thankful to pick up the subject of weather. "Every day has been beautiful since we passed the storm on to the unfortunate people east of us. I have walked into an odd situation here, but I am enjoying the countryside very much."

As they passed the driveway to Roland's cottage they saw Maybelle waiting with Teddy to cross the road. Clio waved and the child whooped and gestured with both arms. Maybelle was smiling.

"You have some friends there," Mr. Stamford remarked.

"Yes. They give me a warm feeling. But Mrs. Linville is very hostile. I cannot understand it."

He said, "Look in your mirror."

Not knowing what to reply, she remained silent.

When they passed out of the manor gateway, Mr. Stamford turned the horses south and stepped up the speed. "My home is beyond the river. We must go into Scudderfield to cross the bridge. Am I driving too fast?"

"No," said Clio. "But pray do not take any sharp curves or I shall surely fly out!"

He declared, "Cannot have that happen. Mason will tell you I am a careful driver. He taught me himself. Of course he does not think I am as expert as he." He turned his head. "Isn't that right, Mason?"

"Whatever you say, sir," intoned the groom, staring ahead half a mile.

Clio and the gentleman exchanged smiles and became easier. Evidently Mr. Stamford did not wish to discuss the Linville tangle in the presence of a third party, for he began to talk about his home.

"Father is breeding horses in a small way. He leaves the management of our manor to my elder brother, whose property it will be someday and who was designed by heaven for just such activity. John is not much in the petticoat line. Says he prefers cattle and crops to silly females—present ladies excluded."

"That must disappoint your parents," she said.

It was obvious where the burden for heirs must fall, although this was not put into words by either of them.

"If you have looked across the river from the manor you may have seen our house," he remarked.

"Oh," she exclaimed, "do you mean the Palladian villa that is halfway up the hill?"

"Yes."

"It looks exquisite. By whom was it built?"

He turned the team right and they passed over the bridge before Brill's inn.

"My grandfather began it sixty-five years ago. You see, we are still considered newcomers in the neighborhood."

Outside the inn he slowed to call a cheery greeting to the man lolling on a bench beside the door. "Ho, Peterkin! Don't you think it's too early for ale?"

"Just waitin', sir," returned the fellow, giving a tug to the flaxen shock of hair over his forehead. "It's easier waiting outside where the smells can't make me thirsty too soon."

Mr. Stamford grinned and drove on. "Fellow's always thirsty," he told Clio. He turned his team to the right to a lane along the western side of the river. "Here come two of his mates. Brothers, as you can see from their square jaws."

He slowed the curricle again.

"Sam! Simon! How's your father doing?"

The sturdy men, who wore matching laborers'

smocks, waved. "Mean as his ole self," said one, and the other added, "Must be gittin' well."

As a politician, Mr. Stamford would wish to maintain contact with the people he represented, yet Clio had the feeling that he was truly interested in his constituents. She had no knowledge of government, and Papa's concern with the wrangles of Parliament had been only lukewarm. She could not suppose Mr. Stamford would espouse issues that were anathema to his father, whatever they might be.

On this side of the river the lane rose gently to the point at which they turned into the general's gate. For a few minutes, as they curved upward, the house she had glimpsed from her bedroom window was concealed by trees. Then they broke into an open space and Mr. Stamford reined his team. Mason leaped down. A footman came to meet them, although Mr. Stamford handed Clio to the ground himself.

A smiling lady had come onto the stoop. "There you are!" she said, as if they did not know it. Her dark hair was shot with gray, but her eyes were lively. She wore an afternoon frock of pale amber and a long string of pearls that Clio was sure was real. Before Mr. Stamford could introduce his guest, the lady had exclaimed, "My dear Miss Caldicott, come in at once. The general is feeling cheated at having to wait."

Mr. Stamford cast Clio a rueful glance and shrugged his shoulders. "At least let me present Miss Caldicott to Father," he begged.

"Well, of *course,* dear."

Another footman held open the door and they went as a body through a spacious vestibule into a circular hall floored with white marble. A curving stair rose opposite the door and within its embrace was a graceful statue of Diana. The walls were soft blue. Mr. Caldicott would have approved.

Mrs. Stamford led them through two parlors on the

right and, behind the second, into a study where the master of the house waited impatiently. Clio was conscious of ferocious eyebrows over alert brown eyes and enough vitality almost to eject him from his seat. He wore a gaudy robe with a white scarf tucked casually into the neckline.

"Damn this leg. Can't do the pretty," he growled.

Mr. Stamford said, "Allow me to present Miss Caldicott, Father."

"I know who she is!" the general declared. "Get a chair, Hugh. Get a chair."

His son drew a chair close to the gentleman's stool and splinted leg, and Clio sank onto it, astonished at her reception but entertained by it.

"What is going on over there, hey?"

"Now, General-my-love," interposed Mrs. Stamford calmly, seating herself at a convenient table, "this is not a court of law. We will have a civilized tea first. Ring the bell, Hugh."

General Stamford made a hmphing noise. "No time to be laid up," he complained. "Immobilized! Leg worthless!"

"At least it wasn't shot off," his son said.

"Tea won't cure it," replied the outraged patient unanswerably.

"But will soothe tempers," Mrs. Stamford promised. "Here it is now."

A servant entered and set the tea tray beside his mistress, who began to fill cups.

Clio could not decide which parent was most delightful. Such forthright spirits—and no ill-feeling. She caught the younger Mr. Stamford's eye, and he raised his brows as if to say, *You see? Hopeless.* His affection for his unruly parents was obvious.

Mrs. Stamford asked a few civil questions and it was soon revealed that her guest came from a scholarly background.

"Bookish, eh?" said the general. "Hugh turned in quite a record at Cambridge. Neither of my sons is militarily minded. John, thank God, has his feet on the ground—literally—and not on London pavement!"

Hugh Stamford looked amused and unoffended. "Tell Father and Mama how you happened to come here," he suggested.

This being the whole purpose of her visit to the Stamfords, Clio set aside her cup and briefly sketched her background, life with Mrs. Mellow, and coming to Savaron Manor.

"You poor child!" exclaimed her hostess. "Are you quite alone in the world?"

Clio admitted that she was. "Mrs. Mellow will return in a month or so—I think. I am company for her, you see, and she is very good to me. I am excessively fond of her." She turned from Mrs. Stamford to the general. "She says I can stay with her forever."

No one mentioned that "forever" must mean as long as Mrs. Mellow lived.

"So why did you come here?" asked General Stamford gruffly.

Clio was beginning to think him a jolly old bear. She replied, "For a bit of adventure, sir. It was lonesome in London with Mrs. Mellow away."

"You got more adventure than you contemplated," Mr. Stamford pointed out.

"I cannot believe the Linvilles would be unkind," Mrs. Stamford said with a slight frown.

"Oh, not that!" protested Clio. "It is only that they do not want me there. What little I do that is helpful someone else could do equally well. Everyone is perfectly civil—except Helen Linville."

Mr. Stamford inserted, "Hostile."

His mother nodded vigorously. "Married above herself."

"Now, love—" warned the general.

"I know what I know, and you know it, too," declared Mrs. Stamford, undeterred. "Jealous cat."

Clio looked surprised. "Of me? Why, she's a *Linville*."

"No, she only married one—that easily led Roland. They met when he took his father to High Harrowgate for the waters. She was living there and thought at first she might get the heir, not knowing about Malcolm, you see. Even so, it was an advantageous match for the daughter of an impoverished clergyman—oh, very worthy, I am sure, but not—"

"Wife!"

"—cultured. I was going to say 'genteel' but I suppose you prefer 'cultured,'" she finished irrepressibly.

General Stamford shook his head in fond despair.

His son smiled and said mildly that, without being uncharitable, they could agree that Helen was jealous of her position and wished everyone to acknowledge her consequence.

Mrs. Stamford, not yielding at all, said, "Very well, I will yield to your version, but she is going the wrong way about it."

"Let us hear what else Miss Caldicott can tell us," young Mr. Stamford reminded. He held out his empty cup to his mother to distract her.

Clio said slowly, "I understand what both of you are saying. What puzzles—yes, and distresses me—is the absence of grief in family members. No tears from them! Not like servants and villagers."

"My dear girl," boomed the general, "do you not know that English gentry and nobles are trained from birth—in their minds if not their emotions—to rise above trouble, grief, joy, conquest, *et cetera*, and to give the appearance of detachment?"

"Why, General-my-love," objected his wife, "I cried

for days when my mother died and did not care who saw me."

He beamed at her. "Naturally you cried, love, because you are a tenderhearted creature. That proves my next point: whatever a person is, he is *more so* under stress."

"Do you mean," said Clio wonderingly, "that Eleanor, for instance, who seems so stiff and frozen, is only being true to her introverted nature?"

"Exactly!"

"And Helen acts belligerent because her importance is overlooked?"

"Aye."

"Then Roland, who seems truly sensitive, has had to withdraw to nurse his sorrow? And Halloran . . . I can see that I must think more deeply about all this." In reflecting on her own need to be helpful, she suddenly remembered the note in her reticule. "Oh, Mrs. Stamford," she said, drawing it out, "I almost forgot this. A fine helper I have turned out to be! Mrs. Hampden sends her thanks for your beautiful orchids."

Mrs. Stamford accepted the note and laid it aside. "Would you like to see how we raise our orchids?" she asked. Clio indicated eagerly that she would. "Then come along. We will leave the men to apply their minds to whatever evidence they have. You do not despise a walk, do you? The conservatory is behind the far end of the house."

As she led Clio through a series of tasteful rooms, she commented that orchids were truly the most outragous creatures. "The temperature is seldom to their satisfaction—too hot, too cool. Or the mist is not adequate. Will you believe they often hang their heads in an obsequious manner that is infuriating?"

Clio laughed and assured her that her orchids were

behaving beautifully at Savaron House, a credit to their upbringing.

"Here we are," said Mrs. Stamford, opening a door. They stepped inside but did not immediately move forward, for the lady laid a hand on Clio's arm. "My dear, I have wanted to have a private word with you . . . to warn you about Halloran."

"You are not the first," the girl replied, beginning to feel a certain sympathy for Hal. "No one has told me that he is unprincipled."

"No indeed! Simply a flirt. A shocking flirt. Not to be taken seriously."

"Shall I promise you that I will not do that? To me he seems a little sad."

Mrs. Stamford exclaimed, "Sad!"

"Handsome, bright, lighthearted—at least on the surface. But never taken seriously—trying to find a place in life."

"Well don't, I beg, endeavor to find it for him!" cried her hostess.

"No, no," laughed Clio. "Lady Cora intends to do so. She is here, did you know? She says I am not to worry as she will 'take him in hand.' "

"Two smashing people," Mrs. Stamford said meditatively. "Could they, I wonder, smash each other?" She gave herself a little shake. "Beware of rakes, my dear. You sound like you have a head on your shoulders, but charm is hard to resist."

"Who wants to charm *me*? I scarcely have two shillings to rub together and absolutely no influence with anyone."

"That is what I have been trying to make you see. Halloran wants—must—charm everyone he encounters. It's a matter of necessity to him."

"Yes," said Clio, "I do see, and that is why I think his situation is sad. The one thing that he enjoys is the adventure of archaeology, and Lady Cora has not much sympathy for that."

Mrs. Stamford actually moaned. "My dear girl! You frighten me. How old are you? Nineteen? You sound like a witch!" Thereupon she gave Clio a hug to prove she thought no such thing.

Clio laughed and said she must blame Papa who talked to her about whatever interested him. Never child-talk nor lady-talk.

"Did you have no childhood?" asked the lady, scandalized.

"I suppose not—but I never missed it, not knowing what it might have been. I practice no magic. I hope you will believe that there are a great many things about which I am fearfully uncertain."

A sigh escaped Mrs. Stamford. "I am glad to hear that for I cannot bear perfection in anyone. Do say you will come to me if you are ever troubled!"

Feeling close to tears, though truly grateful, Clio said, "I will. Yes. Thank you!"

"Now let us forget these willful orchids," Mrs. Stamford said bracingly. "It may be time for sherry and I think I am ready for some, whether it is time or not, aren't you?"

The Stamford men were deep in talk when they returned, but welcomed the ladies graciously. Mrs. Stamford stopped at the bellpull to summon a servant. Evidently it was a customary afternoon signal, for a footman soon entered with a tray of glasses and decanter.

Conversation became general, and Clio, wishing to do her part socially, asked if there were any points of interest or historical value in Scudderfield.

"Not a one," declared the general happily.

"Oh, be fair, General-my-love," objected his wife. "The Fielding house on High Street is considered a gem of Late Stuart architecture. Scholars from the universities are always coming to look at it. Still in use, if you please."

"It would not please me," he retorted. "It is very close quarters."

"Four rooms and an attic," she explained to Clio, "but a great deal of atmosphere. When you are raising a family, charm and atmosphere do not mean much, I fear."

Mr. Stamford intervened to tell Clio that Roland and Helen had made their home in the Fielding house when they first married. "Not many houses are available in a small town like Scudderfield. It was thought convenient for Roland to live near the Royal Bank—yes, that is what Sir Linville named it!—which is just across the street."

"High-flown nonsense," said the general. "A *royal* establishment in a puddle of town like Scudderfield? Perhaps it was meant to convey stability."

"That is just what it did, Father," said Mr. Stamford. "From all I can discover the bank is very sound."

"No chance for nefarious motives there?"

"I think not. Lady Linville and Edward Hampden were on excellent terms, and Roland was never one to make ripples. Sir Linville left his wife in charge and she had the utmost confidence in Edward."

"When did Roland move his family to the cottage at the manor?" asked Clio, more interested in people than in banks.

"Eleanor and Edward and their child were living there," replied Mrs. Stamford. "It is a small house, but quite comfortable for Eleanor's little family. Sir Linville died just before Roland's second child was born. *They* were overflowing into High Street, so the Hampdens went along to the dower house with Lady Mary, and the young Linvilles moved to the cottage."

Clio shook her head doubtfully. "All crowded together, and there are half-a-hundred rooms sitting empty at the Hall! What were Lady Linville's feelings? She was accustomed to spaciousness—and suddenly she hadn't enough room to bend her arms."

"Modest staff, too," added Mrs. Stamford.

Her son said, "Miss Caldicott, you must remember I told you that the family takes pride in the Linville name. Malcolm has the title now and I honestly do not think the others are jealous—excepting Helen, who doesn't matter. They simply want very much to remain, be known as the Linvilles of Savaron Manor."

"It is difficult to believe they would *not* be jealous," Clio said hesitantly.

"Primogeniture is the way of life in England," reminded the general. "Law, too."

His wife said, "Yes, and riffs and rows are common enough. Murder also, I think. Kings and princes have set us a fine example!"

Hugh Stamford grinned. "You sound bloodthirsty, Mama, or craving excitement. I do not think we have a conspiracy here." His face sobered. "Yet we must be sure. Lady Linville was a kind and gracious lady. If anyone harmed her, the truth must be discovered and the guilty party apprehended and punished—yes, Miss Caldicott, no matter who it is."

"Hear, hear!" approved the general, slapping his good knee.

"I hope—oh, I don't know what to hope," Clio said.

"Hope for the best," advised Mrs. Stamford. "Pass the sherry again, Hugh."

Clio, however, had noticed the bronze elephant on the mantel and discovered it to be a clock. "Oh, I must go. I must. By the time we reach Savaron Manor I will have been absent two hours, and that is no way to be helpful!"

Mr. Stamford's curricle was ordered, and in a shower of cordial farewells from the Stamfords, she thanked them for their kind reception of her. How much warmer was the welcome here, she thought, than at the dower house.

As she took her seat in the curricle, Clio looked across the river valley—a pleasant view—and saw plainly, a little upstream, the thick line of shrubbery atop the cliff, and to the right of that the masonry of the lookout wall. Might someone here have seen Lady Linville on the fatal evening?

Mr. Stamford took his place beside her, and Mason sprang behind. On the way down the driveway she asked carefully, "Was Lady Linville seen from here?"

His head snapped toward her. "Good God! How did I fail to think of that?" Remembering interested ears behind them, he added smoothly, "The view of Scudderfield is particularly pleasing from this direction, do you not think?"

Clio cooperated with the change in subject by asking if the church was as old as the Fairfield house, saying she would like to see both.

"Easy enough, he answered. "Will take two minutes."

After crossing the bridge, they followed the main road into the small town and were soon slowing before the church. In clear light it looked mellow, comfortable, and reassuring. The wall around the church and graveyard was low enough that Clio could see a weathered assortment of crosses, stelae, urns. An aura of peace hung over the place. Even the laurels that had seemed lowering by night were benevolent now.

"Would you like to go inside?" Mr. Stamford asked.

She shook her head, and he drove onward.

"You see the road begins to rise a few feet and hence becomes High Street," he said. "The term 'High Street' is used in many English villages. This is as near to eminence as Scudderfield can attain in a river valley. Behold the Royal Bank."

The curricle halted before a stone building, rather

severe of line and unembellished save for a heavy oaken door, paneled and carved. As the bank faced away from the sun, and its door was recessed, the design of carving could not be discerned.

Mr. Stamford said, "You must come some morning and examine the fruit and donkeys."

"Donkeys!"

"I swear. Only the carver knows for sure. There is the Fielding house across the way."

"So tiny!" she exclaimed. "Did your mother say four rooms? No wonder they had to move, with two children and now three."

"The cottage Roland and Helen have now is not much larger."

Mr. Stamford drove forward to where an intersecting street gave him meager space to turn his vehicle. Clio waited without speaking until he had managed this maneuver. When they were rolling north again toward Savaron Manor, she said, "Perhaps Helen is cross because she is crowded and thwarted. Will that family continue in the cottage? And the Hampdens in the dower house?"

"I cannot say. Roland has no place to go unless his income permits him to build something. I am afraid Helen will want a house grander than he can afford. As for Eleanor, Malcolm will never put her from the dower house, but Edward Hampden has strict principles. I imagine he may insist upon removing his family."

"What about Halloran?"

Hugh Stamford shot her a quick glance. "Oh, Hal will soon be off to distant climes."

Ten

While Mason held the horses, Mr. Stamford conducted Clio to the door of the dower house. Once out of earshot, he said softly, "I will meet you tomorrow or, at latest, next day."

There was no time for more. As he raised a hand to the knocker, the door was drawn open by Lady Linville's footman.

Clio said a confused thank-you to both and entered. Her escort was already descending the steps.

In the hall she was confronted by Halloran, who demanded to know if she realized she had been gone at least two hours.

"And why not?" queried Lady Cora, coming up behind him. "Is Miss Caldicott a slave of the Linvilles?"

He grumbled that it was time for tea.

"Have tea if you wish," she said cordially. "I prefer sherry myself."

"I mean," Hal explained impatiently, "it is tea *time*. Of course I want sherry. Come along, ladies. We can split hairs just as well in the library. What would you like to drink, Miss Caldicott?"

"I've already had both," she said, removing her bonnet and draping her shawl over one arm as they swept her toward the other room.

Hal said in that case he would have two sherries.

"Do you mean two glasses with sherry or one glass

twice-filled?" asked Mr. Hampden, who was pouring
He handed Lady Cora hers.

"Both. That is, either."

The whole family had assembled: Eleanor, her husband, and Mark, Roland, Helen, looking handsome
in black silk, Teddy and Miss Susan, age three. Master
Colston Linville, not quite six months, was sleeping in
a basket in the pantry while Maybelle had her supper
in the kitchen. Were meals never served at the cottage?

Clio slipped into a window seat and watched with
interest as Lady Cora settled beside Edward and began
to question him about crime in Scudderfield. Clio
thought it daring—even outrageous—for her to utter
the word. However, no one showed any discomfort, so
apparently they did not associate crime with themselves.

Teddy soon joined Clio in the window seat, snug-
gling up to her. She put an arm around him, thinking
he was quite the dearest little fellow. Miss Susan Linville, more shy, but not wanting to be left out of anything good, toddled over to join them just as Teddy
asked, "Where did Gammy go?"

"To heaven," Clio answered softly.

"Hebben," repeated Susan in a piercing treble.

Clio glanced nervously at Helen Linville, but she
was describing to Eleanor the removal of red silk roses
from the sleeves of her frock and had no interest in
what might be transpiring in the window alcove.

Roland had heard, however, and strolled over to
stoop beside his small daughter.

"Is she being a nuisance?" he asked in a tone of
voice that showed he was confident of a negative answer.

"Papa! Papa!" chirped Miss Susan, nearly toppling
him over by hurling herself upon him.

"This one is a monkey," he said to Clio.

"What am I, Papa?" demanded Teddy immediately.

"A knight?" suggested Clio.

He considered that. "A 'Sir' like Uncle Malcolm?"

"Not exactly. He is a baronet," said his father. "Remember, you are a wounded knight. Let me see the afflicted arm. Ah, almost healed. In fact, I cannot see the scar."

"That is because you are looking at the wrong arm," Clio said, unable to keep from smiling.

Teddy squealed, "Trick, Papa! Trick!"

Helen turned her head their way, frowned, and resumed her conversation with Eleanor.

The dinner hour approached. Maybelle came to collect Miss Susan, whose table manners were not considered suitable for a proper dinner party, and Master Teddy, whose high-pitched chatter might not appeal to anyone so elevated as an earl's daughter. Lady Cora, who nursed no unreasonable expectations, did not count on dinner at the dower house, under present circumstances, to be formal.

"Loved ones may be forgiven much," she had been heard to say more than once. "Fools I cannot tolerate."

She was wearing gray this evening, rather low-cut, but she had not put on her pink pearls or sapphire pendant, so she could not be faulted for lack of mourning. Eleanor wore black lace. The men were all in black.

Only Clio was a brush-stroke of color at the table, but no one took any notice of her blue frock and she had forgotten it herself. When Halloran turned his eyes her way, it was upon her face that they fastened. He made her feel distinctly self-conscious, and when she caught Lady Cora watching her, she wished she were any place but at dinner at this house.

Lady Cora from time to time tossed a few comments her way which served to demonstrate her ladyship's acceptance of the girl. Having utmost confidence in her own title, Lady Cora snubbed no one, at least no one with whom she dined.

"I would so like to visit the Hall," she said, speaking generally to the group.

Eleanor replied, "It has not changed since you were last here. Halloran will run you up in the tilbury, if you wish. I do not believe I am quite ready to go there—not since the burial . . . although I suppose I must go soon to see about planting on Mama's grave."

"Miss Caldicott has not seen the wonders of Savaron Hall," Hal remarked. "Don't you think she should do so while she is here? Surely it would be proper if I escorted the *two* of you." He cast a wicked glance at Clio. "We can take the dogcart."

"But in this glorious weather I should prefer to walk. It is less than a mile. Do you enjoy walking, Miss Caldicott?"

Miss Caldicott, who did not like to admit she was an indefatigable walker because her papa kept no carriage, said with what calm she could muster that nothing could be more delightful than getting close to nature.

"Well, Halloran, there's your answer," Lady Cora said. "I'm sure I have seen you dangle a lady from each arm before this."

"Double the pleasure," he responded, playing the gallant. "Join us, Helen?"

That, of course, would spoil Clio's enjoyment, but Helen at once said, "On your third arm? Do I walk in front or behind? Other things are surer."

Lady Cora demanded, "What things?"

"Oh—time and tide—and taxes."

"What about truth?" persisted Hal. "And temperance—no, one cannot always count on that. Thirst? Thieves? Tantrums? We don't want those!"

Clio suggested, "Teacups?"

He shook his head. "Breakable. Untrustworthy."

"Tomorrow!" cried Mr. Hampden. "We think it will never come, yet it always does."

Hal bowed to him. "Edward, you win. There is nothing so sure to come as tomorrow, and it has no arms at all."

Helen made a sound of disgust. "I never heard such faradiddle," she asserted.

"But," protested Eleanor, "tomorrow never comes, or else it keeps on coming and coming. Edward, what do I mean?"

"I am not certain, dear. Perhaps if you ladies will leave us to drink our port in pea—er—in quiet, we can work out a solution to the riddle." He was smiling, as were all, excepting Roland's wife.

Was *that* the secret of Helen's disposition? No sense of humor? Hardly, Clio judged, because the lack need not make her so irritable. She was looking quite handsome that evening in her smart black frock, her hair tastefully arranged to soften her sharp features, and her complexion like a cameo. One could see how Roland might have found her attractive, but having gotten what she wanted, specifically Roland, why was she so dissatisfied, unless she wanted more than Savaron Manor could provide? Did Roland ever take her to London for a Season? Her dress had a *couturière* touch that a village seamstress was not likely to supply.

Eleanor led the ladies into the drawing room, and Hood closed off the doors to the dining salon to protect them from what raucous sounds the gentlemen might produce over a glass of port. A faint rumble of voices reached their ears, but no words, interesting or uninteresting.

"If you will excuse me, Mrs. Hampden," Clio said, "I will finish some notes left undone this afternoon."

"Oh, let them wait," replied Eleanor casually.

Clio saw Helen purse her lips in disapproval.

"There may be more tomorrow, ma'am," she said.

"True," agreed Eleanor. "Some others came while you were gone this afternoon."

Clio inclined her head and withdrew. As she went back along the hall, Mark passed on his way to the front door without meeting her eyes.

The office was dimly lit by a single lamp near the door. She ignited another upon the desk and sat down to work.

Evidently Eleanor had been there during the afternoon, for there was a stack of opened notes awaiting answers, an assortment of bills, some jotted pages that looked like the beginning of an inventory. As she moved these aside to make room for her own work, Lady Linville's address book came to light. She knew what it was because Eleanor had used it to supply her with addresses earlier. She began to turn the pages swiftly, searching for "M." Sure enough! There it was: "Fran Mellow," with the address at which Clio had lived for nearly two years!

Hugh Stamford would have to believe her now.

How curious it all was! Mrs. Mellow had not recognized the name of "Linville," and the Linvilles had never heard of her kind friend, Mrs. Mellow, yet here was evidence of a connection. Elated, she sat holding in her hands complete vindication.

At that moment Roland entered, his manner surreptitious.

"Only see!" she cried, holding toward him the little book.

He saw at once. " 'Fran Mellow'—my mother's own writing. How glad I am to see this, Miss Caldicott. We will certainly put this into the general's hands."

She said that it was a great load lifted from her spirits. To be under a cloud of suspicion was very painful.

"My dear girl, I apologize for all of us. You will forgive us, won't you, for we have been under a cloud of grief." He added, "It is certainly a mystery why Lady

Linville should want a companion. Obviously she did. I'll tell the others at once."

"Yes, please do," she said.

"May I share a secret first?" He appeared excited, so it was sure to be a good one. "I have heard from your friend, Mr. Rawl, and he writes that he will stop on his way to Chippenham, perhaps tomorrow or the next day. He set ten o'clock as the time to expect him."

She clapped her hands. "Oh, wonderful!"

Roland beamed. "I advised his coming directly to the loft, halting his carriage in the stable yard where my mother's groom will see to it."

"This is truly good news. I never thought he would come so soon."

"The trip to Chippenham has something to do with it. Now, promise you won't tell. The others would not give me a moment's peace—deluging me with advice and criticism."

"This will wake them up. Of course I won't tell."

"Won't tell what?" asked Halloran, from the doorway.

Clio's mouth dropped open, and Roland said quickly, "That I loathe working at the bank."

"Oh," said Hal, losing interest, "everyone knows that. What you ought to do is come along with me to Greece."

"I would like to paint Greece and her islands," Roland admitted ruefully. "You forget I have a wife and three children."

"Chains," said Hal callously. It had the sound of an old argument between them.

"Ones I chose," Roland said stolidly.

"But you cannot imagine the quality of the light in Greece!" Hal shrugged. "To each his own. Well, get up, Brother. You are wanted for whist in the drawing room."

Roland shook his head. "I've no mind for cards.

You don't need me. There are four of you, not counting Edward."

"Lady Cora is going to play to us while we risk our all for penny stakes. Edward is reading. Come along."

Roland rose to his feet, handing Halloran the address book. "Look at this. Under 'M.' "

Hal took the little book and opened it impatiently to the "M" section. "Good God. Mellow!"

"Mama wrote it herself. Have you any doubt now that she asked Miss Caldicott to come? Bring it along to show the others."

The two men left the room, quite forgetting the uninvited guest who was hugging herself and thinking General Stamford would surely let her return to London after this. If that was what she *wished*.

Lady Linville's address book brought astonishment to those waiting in the drawing room. Lady Cora deserted the piano to lean over Eleanor's shoulder. Edward came from the library.

There it was in good black ink: "Fran Mellow."

"In our mother's writing," Hal pointed out.

"Yes," said Helen slowly, "hers, but she could be caught in some crooked scheme."

Mr. Hampden said, "Could, but it is highly unlikely that she was. In any case, we know Miss Caldicott had nothing to do with Lady Linville's death, as she was not here when it occurred. Give me the address book. I'll see that General Stamford gets it in the morning." With that, he retired to the library and the newspapers in which he had been immersed.

Lady Cora resumed playing soft music and the card game proceeded erratically.

Meanwhile, Clio had retreated to her chamber where Molly, called from across the hall, unbuttoned the back of Clio's blue dress.

"The others are playing whist, but I think I will go to bed early," she said to Molly in a friendly manner.

"Yes, miss. It's been trying for everyone."

"Well, I for one couldn't keep my mind on cards. You might think a half-grown boy like Mark would like a game, but he went off somewhere."

Molly took the bait. "Oh, *him!*" she said with such a wealth of innuendo that Clio dared the next question.

"He wasn't at dinner the night Lady Linville fell, was he? I think someone mentioned that."

"No'm," sniffed Molly. "Cold drunk on his bed, he was."

Startled, Clio exclaimed, "You saw him?"

"No'm. But I smelt the fumes when I slipped up to light chamber lamps. I backed out of there, I did!"

When had he reached his room? Who was to say? Wisely, she did not ask details, except, "Has this happened before?"

"Aye," said Molly.

"I wonder if his parents realize," Clio murmured.

"Him's too busy, her's besotted," Molly opined, turning down the covers of Clio's bed efficiently.

Long acquaintance with her father's students led Clio to say like an oracle, "That boy ought to be in school."

"Oh, no, miss," replied Molly, hands on hips, eyes rolling heavenward. "He might catch a headcold or not get enough to eat."

Clio clapped her hands to her mouth to smother a giggle, and Molly danced out the door with a flirt of striped skirts.

Wherever Mark went, he had to return before Hood locked the house for the night, or he had a key, or an accomplice, or some secret entrance. None of these seemed likely.

She decided she could not solve the matter tonight. Let Mr. Hugh Stamford do it! But she would remember to investigate whether there was a tree or a trellis that Mark might climb to reach his room.

Eleanor and Lady Cora ascended together after tea at about ten. Clio was still awake and heard their muted voices saying "sleep well" to each other. Mr. Hampden followed ten minutes later. And then Hood passed her room on his way to the attics.

There was no sound of Mark's arrival. If roving was his habit, presumably his stealth had been perfected.

As for Roland and Helen, they had only a short walk home. And a mile stroll in the dark would be nothing for one who, like Halloran, had known every inch since his birth.

How different her life had been from theirs!

The next day, Wednesday, everyone overslept. It was the fault of a dilettante sun and weeping clouds. The shrubs at the cliff's edge were only a gray mass, with nothing visible beyond. A light rain, falling upon despondent leaves, coasted to the ground where grass thirstily drank it up and grew more energetically than the gardener could like.

The noise of Mr. Hood and the footman, coming down from the attics, awakened Clio. Groping for her watch, she read eight-fifteen and leaped from her bed just as Molly came in with hot water.

"I'm at sixes and sevens, miss, what with oversleeping," Molly apologized. "I hope you wasn't feeling forgot."

"No, just ashamed of being lazy."

"Never fear. Miss Eleanor hasn't stirred and Mr. Edward, who is always early down, hasn't showed or rung."

"Emotional exhaustion, I expect," Clio said, pouring some of the water into her bowl.

"Will you be needing help with buttons, miss?"

"Not today, thank you."

"Cook overslept, too, miss, so breakfast will be a mite delayed. Shall I bring some tea or chocolate?"

Clio shook her head. "I'll have something when I come down. You run along and forget me."

Molly curtsied and whisked out the door.

This was no day for a walk to the Hall. To cheer herself Clio chose a bright yellow frock with an aster-bronze sash just below the bosom and a bow at the center with ends falling nearly to the floor. *I do not have enough variety for a week,* she thought ruefully, *and only one dinner gown, for which there is no use. Well, very likely no one will notice.*

Halloran, who might have done so, was not at the table, being ensconced in the Hall. Naturally Mark was sleeping. Mr. and Mrs. Hampden were on the stair just ahead of her, and by the time the three reached the dining salon, Lady Cora could be heard descending.

"Good morning, Cora," Eleanor greeted her as she seated herself.

Lady Cora chose a seat to Edward's right and said, "I would not call it good. Halloran will be wishing himself in the Mediterranean."

Eleanor murmured that constant sunshine could be tiresome. "If you still want to visit the Hall, you can take Mama's carriage."

Hood set eggs and gammon before Lady Cora, and the footman offered her a choice of toast or muffins. "Oh, I have not despaired of sunshine today," she replied, viewing her plate with satisfaction. "Every now and then a ray breaks though."

It was true, as Clio discovered in a brief glance at the window. She both wanted and did not want to accompany Hal and Lady Cora. The prospect of seeing the wonders in the baronet's mansion was exciting, but she could not like being thrust into the office of chaperone for those two dashing persons.

Before they had finished eating, Hal was there in the flesh. "Came down in your carriage, Cora. Hope you did not mind my subjecting your team to a sprinkle."

At that moment the heavens responded with a sudden downpour.

"Never fear," he added. "The whole rig is safe in Mama's stable. I'll have some coffee, thank you, Hood."

Lady Cora, who appeared unmoved by the fate of her groom, horses, and stylish traveling chaise, remarked, "Do you know it is nearly two years since I set foot in the Hall. I have many happy memories of it and shall have to visit your playroom. Do you recollect how we all drove your governess mad?"

"Eleanor and Roland were docile children," Hal corrected with a laugh. "Only you and I set the poor creature in a panic."

"I was older," Eleanor reminded them, "and seldom part of your romps."

"And Roland never caused trouble," Hal added.

Halloran had told Clio that Lady Cora was a beauty from birth. She wondered what sort of nature she had had as a child. A cozening minx, she suspected.

"I forbid you to expose me to Miss Caldicott," Lady Cora said sternly, a smile pulling at her mouth.

"Well," said Eleanor, "Miss Caldicott and I will work in the office while you two try your incantations on the sun." She was beginning to sound more human, Clio thought.

"And I," announced Mr. Hampden, pushing back his chair, "am off to the bank, while you three dawdle shamelessly."

Eleven

As Clio followed Eleanor Hampden across the hall to the office, her turbulent thoughts jumped from the rain to Mr. Stamford to what time and where. Since he had not been specific, she could only assume he meant the time and place they had met before, and that was midmorning at the overlook. If not today, he had said, tomorrow. Well it was drizzling intermittently. She doubted he would come, and if he did, surely he would not expect her in this weather. But she was anxious to learn what new information he might have uncovered.

Eleanor handed her a sheaf of bills, asking her to sort them chronologically and see if she could determine which had been paid. "We will toss out all the old ones," she said. "You will find some are marked 'paid.' My mother was usually careful about that."

It was quite a thick pile. To find most of the bills still pending would have shocked the careful Clio, but she soon was able to set aside the majority.

"Here is one with a note from an apothecary thanking Lady Linville for her gift to his little daughter."

"Oh, yes. Mama sent the child a toy when she fell from an apple tree and broke her collarbone."

"Everyone seems to have liked your mother," Clio ventured.

"Do you think so? She was a marvelous person, really. Always doing things for people. Of course she was absentminded about little things. I mean, important facts never escaped her. Such a contradiction! Well, for instance, she never forgot a promise of help, although she seldom remembered if anyone owed her a debt. I cannot count the times she said 'generosity is a farce if it expects repayment.' Not that she was careless about business! Edward says she was wonderful to work for because she understood banking problems so thoroughly."

"Did it not take a special sort of talent to keep several families happy in such close quarters?"

"In each others' pockets? Us? Why, I suppose so. I never thought about it," Eleanor confessed. "Edward and I came to stay with Mama after Father died, and we just never left. Whenever we mentioned moving there was always some reason against it. And Roland needed our cottage for his growing family. Things just drifted for a while, and then—well, none of us wanted to leave my mother alone. Oh, she was healthy and active, but she wasn't *young*. No, none of us could leave her alone up here."

Clio digested that. She sorted bills deftly, thinking: Six or seven relatives who wouldn't leave her alone— and she wanted a companion!

"What is the matter?" Eleanor asked.

"Matter?"

"You were shaking your head."

"I was? Oh, well, I was thinking how glad I am not to have fifty-pound butcher bills."

Eleanor stretched out her hand. "Let me see. Oh, that is a mistake. Should go to the Hall." She dropped the paper on the floor. "Miss Caldicott! Whatever is wrong with me? We haven't said a word about your salary. . . . Don't bother, dear. I'll get it. Thank you. Now, naturally we expect to pay you for your time with us."

"Oh, Mrs. Hampden, do not worry about me. You have much to trouble—"

"But we must not be unfair."

"Why, you aren't at all. I am eating like a queen and sleeping like a—"

"Is your room truly comfortable? I gave it no thought!"

"Yes. Everything is fine. You must not worry. I am glad to be useful someplace."

There was an awkward pause during which Halloran appeared and hurled himself into a chair. "Being *decorative* ought to be enough," he observed.

Eleanor said shortly, "Do not be personal, Hal. Where is Lady Cora?"

"Nattering with Plummy again. Sorting Mama's clothes, I think. Drat this weather!"

"Is there a wee clearing place in the sky upriver?" asked Clio hopefully.

Hal craned his neck. "Might be, but we need more than that. What are you ladies doing?"

"Accounts," said Eleanor impatiently.

"I'll help, too," said Hal.

"Oh, no you won't, Hal Linville," she retorted. "You are nothing but a nuisance."

"That's sisterly appreciation," Hal explained to Clio.

"Now, Hal, we're busy." Eleanor rattled some papers, adding with a curious emphasis, "Go keep Cora entertained."

"Her ladyship's always entertained."

"Then find some sensible work to do."

He pretended to cringe at the word "sensible" . . . or perhaps it was at "work." In any case, he went away.

"Hal's pestilent," Eleanor said, blending irritation nicely with affection.

Clio added, "Bored."

They worked in silence for a time, until Eleanor,

setting down her pen with a sigh, observed that Halloran should offer for Lady Cora, who would keep him busy for sure.

"Would she accept . . ." Clio began hesitantly and then cut off guiltily, being aware of her own tenuous place.

Eleanor looked surprised. "Well, of course. That is, I think so. Mama wished for the union, and Cora's mother wishes it also. Do you not think they make a handsome couple?"

Handsomeness did not seem to Clio to be the main point in matrimony. Should not there be some meeting of minds? Some shared interests? Some *affection*? She ventured mildly, "There is Lady Cora's title. Perhaps he hesitates to ask her to—to step down."

"But she would not step down!" corrected Eleanor. "She would not lose her title and Linville is a respected name. It is common knowledge that she has already refused gentlemen with titles as good as her own."

Clio admitted to herself that she was no one to judge the matter. However, she could not resist mentioning Halloran's deep interest in archaeology. "I believe he said he is planning to go to the field again soon."

"*When* he obtains backing. I daresay he will forget all that nonsense if he marries Lady Cora. They will entertain and travel and have a very full social life to keep him occupied."

"But archaeology is his chief interest!"

"He will forget it," Eleanor assured her.

"My papa," said Clio slowly, "had the same ambition. But he was obliged to give it up in order to take care of me. It makes me sad to think about it."

Eleanor frowned in concentration. "Was he unhappy?"

"I don't know. He kept me from knowing. He was a very good father." Clio's voice trembled a bit at the last, and Eleanor hastened to say, "My dear! I am so sorry." She hesitated, then added. "Every situation cannot be just like another."

"I hope not!" declared Clio. Her inflection was not lost on Eleanor, who said no more.

The bills blurred before Clio's eyes, as she wondered if anyone cared about Halloran's feelings. She would have to talk with him more—in detail—to determine if digging for ancient treasures was truly his aim in life or only a sort of escape. Any wife worth her salt would accompany him in his true career.

Both ladies worked diligently until summoned to nuncheon, at which time it was discovered that Hal and Lady Cora had some magic powers, for the sky was surely clearing. Hal observed that they might well go to the Hall after eating.

Lady Cora was undaunted by dripping trees, although wet roads and paths led her to suggest that they ride to the Hall in her chaise. "After all, it is waiting right here to be of use, and the interior of the Hall is what Miss Caldicott wishes to see. *That* will be dry, you know."

Clio did not want her "wish" to be responsible for everyone's activities. She demurred, reminding them that Lady Cora desired to visit the childhood playroom.

"I can't understand this playroom notion," said Hal. "Just shabby toys and faded covers on the chairs! Aren't you getting old for dolls, my pet?"

Lady Cora tossed her head. "A female is never too old for dolls. Will Cheops still be there? I shall like to see how you respond to him."

"Cheops!" exclaimed Clio. "Is he a doll, or a soldier, or a bear?"

"A bear?" cried Hal, defending his boyhood treasure. "If you are your father's daughter, you must know he was a great king of Egypt."

Stung, she retorted quickly, "Indeed I do know who he was, but I cannot expect to meet him in the playroom of Savaron Manor of England!"

Hal grinned. "The essence of him, you can. You will see. Cheops! I hadn't thought of him for an age. Do not give away the secret, Cora!"

"Ah!" said Edward, pouncing verbally. "Playing games like children. How old are you now, Hal? Twenty-six? And you, Cora? Roland and I have more serious matters to attend to. Are you coming to the bank this afternoon, Roland?"

Roland and Clio exchanged guilty glances. Neither's anticipated visitor had come that morning. Only one was expected by both; the other had not exactly promised . . .

"Might as well," Roland said. "Are you riding?"

Edward shook his head. "Muddy. Let us take the dogcart, since Cora has her chaise."

After a nibble of cheeses, the two went out via the kitchen and vegetable rows, passing the word to Lady Cora's groom that she was ready for her carriage.

When Hal arrived at the Hall with his two ladies, word reached the housekeeper by some mysterious route, and she was waiting for them in the entrance hall as soon as they came up the steps. Two footmen and two maids were ranged behind her, all presenting smiling faces. It was clear that her ladyship was popular here. With bows and curtsies they welcomed her, none of them young. It seemed likely to Clio that they had been here for all Lady Cora's visits over the years and held her in honest affection. While Lady Cora went from one to another, calling each by name, Hal presented Mrs. Pratt to Clio.

"Mrs. Pratt," he explained, "was allowed to stay on for Sir Malcolm because the Hall could not operate without her. Pratt was under-butler under Hood and was elevated to butler when Hood joined Mama at the dower house. Is your husband doing his job, hey?"

"In bed with a cough just now, sir, but otherwise he's satisfactory," smirked Mrs. Pratt.

"I knew it!" said Hal. "You hold him to the mark."

The woman curtsied to Miss Caldicott and bid her welcome, to which Miss Caldicott, in a composed manner that won Mrs. Pratt's approval, replied with a warm smile and thanks. The welcome she received from all was pleasant and genuine, yet Clio thought the enthusiastic reception of Lady Cora made it plain that all wished Cora for Halloran's wife.

Eleanor was right. They did make a handsome couple.

"We have brought Miss Caldicott to see the Hall," said Lady Cora. Undoubtedly, news of Miss Caldicott had reached the Hall days ago, and the mystery of her arrival had been much discussed in the servants' dining hall. Lady Cora's words and manner, now, conveyed the attitude that must be assumed toward the unexpected visitor.

Mrs. Pratt said, "Certainly, my lady." She dismissed the other servants, evidently intending to lead the tour herself, and asked if they would like to begin at once.

Lady Cora said they would.

Clio soon discovered that a mixture of exteriors had produced a corresponding interior hodgepodge. She found all interesting, if not always beautiful. By taking her cue from anything that Lady Cora, Hal, or Mrs. Pratt called to her attention, she succeeded in declaring certain things "handsome," "impressive," "very fine," "outstanding," and "most graceful." She varied her comments from room to room, although she almost ran out of suitable adjectives.

So many rooms and so richly furnished! Clio felt sure that the servants she had seen were only a few of the total needed to maintain the Hall in such excellent condition. All spoke of money and wealth, and she wondered how much Hal's father had been able, with the establishment of a bank, to provide for his children by Lady Mary.

Lady Cora's obvious satisfaction with what they saw caused Clio to suspect that her own home—that is, the earl's principal residence—was in the same style. Perhaps the same was true of the property Lady Cora described as "my manor outside London." The general effect here was very good, even elegant, but Clio preferred the restrained taste of Lady Linville's dower house. She wondered a bit that Halloran, with his love of things Greek and Roman, could consider these ornate rooms beautiful. The answer must be that in looking at *this* he saw no details, but simply his home.

By the time they had reached the portrait gallery, Lady Cora was noticeably restless. "I cannot look at all these faces," she declared. "Let us go to see my old chamber, Mrs. Pratt, while Hal shows Miss Caldicott the various paintings. Hal, you will want to introduce her to your ancestors, will you not?"

Mrs. Pratt's face revealed a new interest in Clio. She said disapprovingly, "If you wish, my lady."

"I do wish. What would you say, Hal, if we meet for tea in the old playroom? With a fire in the grate, Mrs. Pratt."

"Jolly idea," agreed Hal, "only let us have chocolate as we did when we were children."

While the housekeeper went into the hallway to give instructions to a servant, the visitors drifted inside the gallery.

"Do you think me whimsical, Miss Caldicott?" asked Lady Cora. "Savaron Hall has been my second home, but in recent years I have not entered it except when invited to dine with Malcolm and his wife. This chance to explore is irresistible."

"I am certainly not resisting," Clio answered with a smile, "and Mr. Linville's vocation is exploring."

Hal drew out his watch and asked, "How long till we meet?"

"Twenty minutes? No, Mrs. Pratt and I shall want to have a coze. Let us say half an hour."

Mrs. Pratt returned to carry off Lady Cora, and Halloran said to Clio, "You won't want to examine every portrait. It would require much longer than half an hour. Shall I choose the most notorious? Let us begin at the left. They are arranged chronologically." By a light touch to her elbow he guided her to the nearest portrait.

The gentleman before them had a strong face and eagle eye. "He founded the family fortune," said Hal. "I have always thought it was by piracy."

"Boyhood fantasy," objected Clio.

"No-no. You will notice he wears a sword, and there is no record of his serving in any army. Look at the next, his third wife. Mousy enough, wouldn't you say? But she must have had endurance for she outlasted him by fifteen years."

"That meek lady!"

"Looks deceive. We poor gentlemen must guard our hearts and use our heads." He gave her a saucy glance.

She thought he spoke truly. It was common knowledge that men sought wives who had money or beauty or both. They cared little for what was inside female heads. Of course, she admitted to herself, girls who had families to barter for them might hold out for wealth and station. It was orphans like herself who had no expectations.

Halloran interrupted her thoughts by muttering, "Good God. A chaperone."

"What?"

He gestured toward the far end of the room where

a manservant in a serviceable apron had appeared
with bucket and rags to polish windows.

"Insulting. Well, these pictures cannot interest you.
The terrace looks dry. Let us walk out there in the
sun. That will certainly be public enough!" He opened
a door and ushered her outdoors, grating, "Mrs. Pratt
is getting above herself."

Clio's cheeks were pink and she was glad of a light
breeze to cool them. If Lady Cora had blithely abandoned them alone in the gallery she must think it no
way improper. For the housekeeper to send a servant
to lend them countenance was humiliating for both.

To soothe Halloran's offended self-respect, she said
lightly, "You were thoughtful to suggest this. The sunlight and balmy air are so welcome after dispiriting
rain."

"Aye," he agreed. Then he said, "Glorious clear air
in Greece."

"You miss it."

He led her in a gentle stroll along the terrace.

"I had forgotten," he said at last, "how one's family—one's longtime servants—will not allow one to
mature."

"Is it not a sign of affection?"

"Perhaps. But so lowering."

Neither said anything as they turned and retraced
their steps along the flags.

"I wish I knew what to do," he burst out at last.
"Everyone belittles my dreams. Now that my mother
is gone I have no *tie* except the damnable disapproval."

"Well, go!" exclaimed Clio.

He looked at her in surprise, having almost forgotten her presence. "My roots are here," he explained
slowly.

"And where," she demanded, "are your branches
and leaves?"

He halted and seized her arm. "My dear Miss Caldicott, I thank you! Where indeed? Some decisions are in order. Just answer me one more question. What sort of woman would venture hundreds of miles away to heat and dirt and strange food?"

A little dizzied by her own boldness, she said, "One who cared."

"Cared? Of course, cared!" His eyes began to gleam. "But first we must put the *playroom* behind us." His hold on her arm tightened. "Come along, Miss Caldicott. Oh, I do hope Cheops is still there!"

Reaching the playroom necessitated returning to the main hall, mounting the great oaken stairway, passing along a broad passage flanked by closed doors, and ascending another stair which was steep but lighted by a high, dormer window. She was allowed to grasp a handrail while Halloran climbed behind her.

At the top of this flight lay a wide landing where Lady Cora was waiting.

"Here you are," exclaimed Lady Cora. "I feel six years old again! Imagine the servants having to climb all those stairs with coals and nursery meals, not to mention taking down dishes and ashes!"

Clio was puffing, for Halloran had hurried her, but he was not winded.

"I say, Cora, what a splendid idea. Why have we not done this before?"

"I have opened a window for some fresh air and the fire makes it seem like old times."

Clio was amused that her ladyship felt no concern for the servant just then coming up with chocolate and biscuits.

They entered the room and stood looking about.

"Good God," said Hal. "Where are the old curtains with violets? And the lumpy cushions?"

"Those have been replaced, making things pleasant for Malcolm's children, Mrs. Pratt says. Let us have

our chocolate while it is hot and then we can search
for the toys that we remember."

In the grate coals were beginning to turn red, although the fire was not a large one, being needed only
for its cheery aspect. Halloran drew up two chairs for
the ladies and a stool for himself. "I remember," he
said, "when I thought this was a large stool and now
my knees are almost under my chin."

"There is another chair in the corner," Lady Cora
said, pouring the chocolate, "but I must say it does
my heart good to see you subdued for a change." She
handed them cups.

"Subdued?" cried Hal. "Not at all! Miss Caldicott
has given my thoughts a new turn."

"Inspired by portraits of your ancestors or a turn
on the terrace?"

So she had seen them from a window! Clio, who was
guilty of nothing, noted the slight edge to her voice
and colored faintly.

"The ancients are so dull, and the weather improv-
ing," said Halloran, noticing no undercurrents. "I say,
Cora, by the time we finish here, things may be dry
enough for us to walk back to the dower house as we
originally planned. What do you say?"

"I say yes," Lady Cora replied, "so long as I do not
ruin my slippers."

"You ladies affect such perishable shoes," he
teased.

Lady Cora, who seemed to be recovering her verve,
pointed out that he was excessively fond of his boots,
as all the servants knew.

Clio, having no part in this exchange, sipped her
beverage and surveyed the attic with interest. It was a
very large room, with sloping walls painted yellow. It
seemed clean and fresh, but as Lady Cora and Halloran had not commented on the color, she assumed
it had been the same in their day. For the most part,

the floor was bare except for an old rug on the hearth where they sat. There was a chair for rocking babies, and shelves of toys, old and new.

A lull having occurred, she asked if they had found their own favorites.

"My doll is here—the one Eleanor allowed me to mother," said Lady Cora. "I call her Queen Maud. She is still whole, although I cannot like her new gown for it is not twelfth century. Cheops is on the bottom shelf, Hal."

"He is, by Jove." Hal set down his cup and bounded across the room. "Ah. Here. See what you think of him, Miss Caldicott."

She hurriedly returned her cup to the tray and received into her hands a strange wooden object. "Why, he's a *pyramid!*" she exclaimed.

While Lady Cora watched in amusement, Hal announced Cheops was indeed a pyramid, a magic one. He took back the toy, made some mysterious twists and turns on it, and happily displayed an opening in the bottom.

Clio clapped her hands and asked, "The burial chamber?"

"Not that perhaps," he admitted, pleased at her quickness, "but a magic place, a secret chamber."

"Why not put something in it for Malcolm's boys to find," suggested Lady Cora. "A coin?"

He groped in a pocket. "I will put two, one for each boy." He popped the coins into the chamber, made some turns of various parts, and handed the sealed pyramid back to Clio who studied it on all sides but could find no opening.

"What small boy would not like this!" she said admiringly. "Have you ever seen the real thing?"

"Not yet, but I hope to someday."

Clio said wistfully that she wished she might, and

Lady Cora laughed tolerantly and pointed out that Egypt was no place for delicately nurtured ladies.

"Well, now," objected Hal, "the Egyptians have wives, you know."

"And what sort of life do they live?" demanded her ladyship. "Drudgery, I am sure."

"What do you know about it?" asked Hal, becoming hot. "For that matter, what do you know about the poor of England?"

"My father takes excellent care of his people, I'll have you know!" she countered.

"I daresay he does. Fine gent. But what experience have you—or the earl—had with London slums or Nile villages?"

Since Lady Cora had no knowledge or experience of either, she bit her lip. Clio stepped into the gap as peacemaker.

"It is a distressing fact of life that one finds slums all over the globe. We cannot wipe them out everywhere forever. Mr. Lambton at All Souls regularly reminds his congregation that 'the poor ye have always with you.' My papa said we must try to *understand.*" She noticed that the antagonists were growing calmer, so wound up by adding: "If we understand, we may be able to help . . . if only in a small way."

All of this rigmarole had little to do with Hal's going to Greece or Asia Minor, but it distracted the combatants to the extent that they could say nothing.

It was a relief to all when footsteps sounded on the stair and a maidservant came to ask if they wished more chocolate. Lady Cora in her undisputed role of social arbiter said that nothing more was required and that they must go.

They left the maid to close the window and douse the fire, descended to say farewell to Mrs. Pratt, and set off down the driveway, Hal not over-strained by having a lady on each arm.

Twelve

The vicar and his wife had been invited to dinner, not a party, yet a dinner somewhat more formal than previous ones had been. Clio elected to wear her one evening dress, a white muslin with tiny puffed sleeves ending in ruffled embroidery. It exposed a great deal of arm but the neckline was modest.

Molly, who helped her to dress, declared she looked like a lily and all she needed was a flower in her hair. Although Clio protested in a whisper from the top of the service stair, Molly sped down to the garden and returned with a real lily to fasten where Clio's hair was tied back. Neither girl knew if fashionable ladies used lilies this way, but the effect was charming.

"It may wilt a bit, miss, but not before dinner has ended," Molly assured her.

"Suppose I am expected to stay the whole evening?"

"Never you mind. The vicar is a nice old fellow and his wife's a bit balmy. Treated like relatives here. If the flower wilts who's to notice or care?"

Privately, Clio thought Lady Cora would not miss an item of her attire. She would examine discreetly, but thoroughly. Could Clio count on Molly's advice?

"Don't you worry, miss," said Molly, sensing Clio's uncertainty. "I know a lady when I sees her, and Mr. Hal will, too."

"Oh," gasped Clio, flushing, "You must not think

I would attempt to—attempt to—put myself forward
in an *encroaching* way."

"No'm. We know that all right and tight," Molly
assured her. Just who "we" might be Clio was not certain, but she had an uncomfortable feeling that she
had been discussed in the kitchen.

Was the opinion of servants as dependable as Mrs.
Mellow's? She decided that Lady Linville's staff, being
faithful and true, would not mislead her. She thanked
Molly for her help and descended to the drawing
room where the guests had already been received by
Eleanor. Hesitating in the doorway, she saw Hal look
her way. His eyes widened and he gave a slight nod of
approval. Then Eleanor noticed her and called her
forward to meet the strangers.

The vicar's wife, in her seventies, wore a drab gray
frock of uncertain vintage and her hair was a disturbed
fluff of similar color. When Clio was presented she
turned faded blue eyes on the girl, murmured vaguely
"Delighted," and returned her attention to a glass of
sherry, which she held tenaciously. The vicar, who was
not above the conviviality of sherry either, bowed and
added to the muted colors of the carpet by spilling a
drop or two from his glass. He was white-headed, with
a deeply creased brow, and looked benign, which he
was. No doubt rumors of Miss Caldicott had reached
the vicarage, along with the rest of Scudderfield, but
he accepted Clio's presence as he did everything
about Savaron Manor—with interest but devoid of curiosity.

Hood soon called them to the table. A group of
eight, like this, was not easily arranged. Lady Cora, by
precedence, was naturally seated at Mr. Hampden's
right, and Hal for her enjoyment at *her* right. The
vicar's wife was therefore set at Mr. Hampden's left,
with Clio next to her, and then the vicar between Clio
and his hostess. This left Mark between his mother

and Hal. Not an arrangement for especial pleasure to any.

Mr. Hampden did his duty with the conversation, totally unassisted by the vicar's wife. Lady Cora could be counted upon to uphold her corner, and she did so with no appearance of boredom. Not only was she a thorough lady, Clio thought, but also she seemed to have an inquiring mind for others' thoughts. If only she would take an interest in Hal's work, they might achieve a marriage of mutual enjoyment.

Directly across the table was Halloran, who supported Lady Cora's talk with fitful comments, while he watched Clio with some difficulty because of the centerpiece between them. The object of his surveillance was thankful for the floral shield. She had not been asked to prepare it, and if she had been, would have proportioned it lower and longer, not knowing the seating plan. Now she was grateful for the bouquet as protection. Hal, being tall, could see more of her than she could of him. All she saw, when she dared look that way, were his beautiful, caressing eyes. Did he gaze at all women that way? Could he not help it?

Mark, as usual, scarcely raised his eyes from his plate, and Eleanor soon ceased all effort to converse with the dear vicar, who contributed only "True, true" and "Quite so, quite" and "Umm, yes, yes."

It was rather a dismal meal, although the vicarage pair may have enjoyed a richer repast than they would have had at home.

When Eleanor led the ladies toward the Gold Parlor, Clio held back to permit her elders and superiors to walk before her. She was surprised to have Lady Cora drift to her side with a whisper that Plummy wished to talk to her.

"Let me take you to her now," she said.

Startled, Clio said, "Why me? She can have no desire to know me."

"But she does," affirmed Lady Cora. "Come with me." And such was her ladyship's calm assurance that Clio found herself trotting to the stair in the wake of her ladyship's blue satin demi-train.

Where was Plummy's room? Where did she hide herself? Clio did not know. She had assumed that the woman occupied a cubbyhole in Lady Linville's suite, or used a cot in the Lady's dressing room. Would she be received there? Surely not in Lady Linville's own chamber!

She had forgotten the sitting room above the Gold Parlor to which Lady Cora conducted her. Mrs. Plumb was waiting there.

"Evening, my lady. Evening, miss," she said with the merest wisp of a curtsey. She looked real enough now, her face composed. Not alarming. "I'd like to speak with Miss Caldicott alone if you don't mind, Lady Cora."

"Of course you may," replied Lady Cora pleasantly. She nodded encouragingly to Clio and exited, drawing the door closed behind her.

Mrs. Plumb motioned Clio to a seat with all the grace of her former mistress, and Clio sank into it, grateful for its physical support, but wondering how she would escape it.

"I hope you will forgive me, miss, for frightening you four days ago," Plummy began. "You see, I thought you were a spirit—a vision—an angel."

"Me!"

Plummy, a somber figure in black, with thin gray hair, reached across to squeeze Clio's hand. Her face was as lined as Clio remembered, and now these lines rearranged themselves to what was unmistakably a smile. "I thought you were my mistress come back from the dead."

Clio was stunned. "I? You thought . . . but I thought *you* were she!"

It was Plummy's turn to be astonished. "I never resembled my dear lady, but you—it is uncanny—you *do*. Let me show you." She reached into a pocket of her skirt and drew forth a miniature which she held out to Clio.

It was a delicate portrait of a young girl somewhere between fifteen and twenty, gray-eyed, with blond curls framing her face and a cluster of them tumbling to her shoulder. The bone structure of the pretty creature was nothing like Clio's, though as a *type* they matched. Poor Plummy had so grieved and so wished to see her mistress again that she had imagined her.

"Did you know Lady Linville when she was this young?" asked Clio, returning the miniature.

"Oh, yes, miss. I raised her from a babe." Tears sprang from her eyes and she had to brush them away with gnarled fingers.

Clio said gently, "I am so very sorry. Everyone loved her. The accident seemed so unlikely and unreal that when I saw you—whom no one had mentioned—I thought I must have dreamed the whole terrible business. I thought you must be the lady who wrote for me to come."

"Aye. She wrote."

"You knew about it?"

Mrs. Plumb shook her head. "No, but they have showed me the address book, and I believe you."

Clio sighed deeply and slumped back in her chair. "But why, why did she ask me to come?"

"I don't know, miss. My lady kept it from me." She also sighed. "Well, what's done is done. Was it an accident? I wish I could know."

"Mr. Stamford is trying to find the truth. Do you think anyone would want to hurt her?"

Mrs. Plumb seemed to have faced that question, for she answered readily, "No, I don't think that . . . but minds are strange things. No saying what kinks are in someone else's head."

"Where were you when she fell?"

"Let me see. I was here when Fralke came up with her tray. I would have said she was in a gay mood— excited, you know. But she said she wanted a quiet supper to herself. So when she was settled with her meal, I went down the back steps to the kitchen for my own. It must have been about six-thirty. Never saw my lovely girl again."

It was an alibi of sorts. Clio was too kindhearted to probe when Mrs. Plumb was so distressed. How long was she absent from Lady Linville's suite? Did she stay in the kitchen until word came of the accident? How was the Lady found?

Busy with her thoughts, Clio did not realize that she sat silent until Plummy said in a more collected manner, "You mustn't take the Linvilles' troubles on your shoulders, missie. What do you think of the family?"

What did she think? Clio was not sure, and even if sure, she might hesitate to say. "Very kind," she offered finally, "to accept me in odd circumstances."

"Yes. And now they know it was right to do so. Is 'kind' all you can tell me? I think they worried my lady in some ways. 'They all have their problems,' she would say to me. Do you think Miss Eleanor spoils her son?"

"Well, yes, I do," admitted Clio. "But how scandalous for me to judge!"

Plummy smiled crookedly. "I 'spect most of the household is making scandal, then. You would think Mr. Edward would put his foot down with a wham— Miss Eleanor's pa certainly would have done so."

"Was he stern?"

"No. Sensible. Mr. Edward must leave his head in the bank vault."

Clio said doubtfully that he seemed very competent and businesslike, to which Plummy retorted, "*All* business. Comes of being a younger son and wanting to be honored for himself."

"Which he is?"

"Aye, missie. I s'pose you can tell Mr. Roland isn't minded to do business at all."

By this time Clio was so interested in what she could learn from Lady Linville's maid that she forgot to be tactful. "Mr. Roland Linville is something better—a true artist," she said. "It is his wife who puzzles me. I think she loathes me."

Plummy erupted with a snort. "If you had a title she'd like you well enough. There's another wanting attention. Running the vicarage in a high-handed way—which it needs, the poor lady there being butter-brained. Miss Helen's fretting now over the church *fête*, trying to run the whole thing."

"That precious Teddy must take after his papa."

Too soon to tell about the children, was Plummy's opinion. "What about Mr. Hal?" she asked.

Clio shrugged. "Still another wanting a name that matters. I do not understand why the family resists his ambition."

"It's because of Lady Cora. What sort of husband for her, a-digging in the dirt in some heathen place?"

"That's his dream!" Clio objected with spirit.

"Not hers. They could be living high in England— that's what my dear dead lady thought."

And therefore, so thought Mrs. Plumb. Now, Clio understood.

Long years of affectionate dialogue with the Caldicotts' housekeeper had taught Clio how to talk comfortably with a person of the servant class and to respect the opinions of one less educated than herself. What a lot she was storing up to tell Mr. Stamford!

At nine Lady Cora returned to say she was bored to flinders, so she would change places with Miss Caldicott, whom Eleanor wanted to assist with tea. Edward had ordered the carriage for nine-thirty to transport the guests home to the vicarage. Hal and Edward were near to breaking their jaws in an effort not to yawn, she told them.

Because Clio did not suppose she was of any interest to Mrs. Plumb and her ladyship, she said goodnight serenely and went obediently to be of use to Eleanor, who was perfectly capable of pouring tea and simply yearned for another face to look upon.

The vicar's wife was relishing a second cup when the carriage arrived at the door and Eleanor exclaimed in a high falsetto, "I declare! The carriage already!" Immediately Edward and Hal were lifting the visitors to their feet, saying what a shame they must leave and sweeping them from the room.

"Such dear people," whispered Eleanor to Clio. "I declare their goodness exhausts me."

Clio laughed softly.

"I'll be busy in the morning. Sleep late," Eleanor said.

This was welcome news for Clio, since it meant she would have some opportunity to meet Mr. Stamford and learn what he had uncovered. She thought happily that she herself would have things to tell, maybe even Mark's furtive way of entering the house.

Molly was waiting for her when she reached her chamber.

"I thought you would be coming soon," Molly said. "I heard the carriage leave the stable." Clio turned her back and Molly began to unfasten tiny buttons, of which there were many this time. "Why, miss, the lily lasted very well. Why not put it in your water glass?"

"All right. I will. After I have cleaned my teeth. Do you remember to clean yours?"

Molly said hastily, "Oh, yes, miss. Lady Linville was very firm about that. It was a rule." She sighed and added, "We will all miss her ladyship. We wonder if Miss Eleanor will be staying here and if she will want *us.*"

This was not something that Clio had thought about. "Why, surely she will," she said, with doubt creeping into her voice.

Molly shook her head forlornly. "We don't even know who will be living here. I don't think I would like to work for Miss Helen. There are not very many openings in Scudderfield. I might have to look for a situation in Wendel."

"I am sure," consoled Clio, "that everything will be worked out satisfactorily. Even Mrs. Hampden cannot be sure of her next step, but when the will is read and all is decided for the family, they will not forget faithful service."

Molly muttered, "I wisht I could go with you to London."

Surprised, yet touched, Clio said, "I wish so, too, but I do not have a home to take you to share."

"Well, I'd like it," Molly insisted.

"You might not. Truly, you might not. London is vast and exciting," Clio explained, "but it is also dirty and dangerous—specially for young girls. Why, you could walk the streets for months and not see a soul you had ever seen before. Does that not sound lonely?"

"Aye," admitted Molly, "but if Mr. Hood retires, and maybe Cook, it could be lonely here."

"Don't you have family in Scudderfield?"

"Only a sister, miss, and she's across the valley at the general's place."

Clio urged, "Do not give up hope. Miss Eleanor might decide she wants an abigail."

That would be heaven, Molly declared, and Clio resolved to drop a hint in someone's ear. It might help, might it not? She fell asleep wondering whose ear would be most receptive.

Thursday, to the joy of all, dawned diamond-bright. As soon as Clio had gulped breakfast, she hastened to the west terrace to make a critical study, in the most casual manner, of Mark Hampden's windows. There was nearby a large beech with widespread limbs that were eminently climbable. Unfortunately, or fortunately, no branch approached close to either window. She also discovered a stout vine climbing adjacent to the window farthest from Mr. Hampden's window and therefore least apt to attract his attention. She drifted twice past the vine and spied no broken tendrils or crushed leaves. Besides, she told herself, the pudgy Mark was unlikely to have sufficient agility to make the climb.

She was just saying to herself, "I believe I could do it—" when a sunny voice asked: "Can you play?"

She swung around. "Oh! Teddy! I did not hear you come."

"I tiptoed," he explained, delighted. "Can you play?"

It was not much more than nine-thirty. "For a while."

They went off hand and hand to sit under Teddy's special tree where Clio, plucking a long leaf of grass, showed him how she could stretch the piece between her thumbs and make a whistle. He grasped the knack at once, and the louder the whistle the more he squealed with excitement. It was a trick she had learned from children in Hyde Park.

When Teddy's excitement was beginning to boil over, she distracted him by suggesting he look for different sorts of leaves. These he brought to her happily, and they talked about each one—its color, shape, or size.

"Why are some large and flat?" he asked.

She answered solemnly, "I suppose so that elves can stand under them to keep dry when it rains."

Teddy was round-eyed. "If I came out in the rain, do you think I might see them?"

"Oh, I doubt it. Elves are very timid, you know."

From where they were sitting Clio could see a portion of the vegetable garden and the gateway to the stable yard. Beyond this, the view was blocked by a traveling chaise, so Clio knew Mr. Rawl had called upon Roland. That meant her own visitor could be waiting.

"I have an errand now, Teddy. Will you meet me here another time?"

"This afternoon?"

"If I am free. Maybe tomorrow."

"Come soon," he begged. "Mama never has time to play."

That simple statement wrung her heart. She watched him dart from under the tree and start across the lawn, skipping on one foot now and then in exuberance. As the happy child neared the terrace, from which a path led off to the left to Roland Linville's cottage, Clio rose to her feet and brushed her skirt. She saw Helen Linville come from the terrace door and meet Teddy. The next moment Helen had seized her son by his arm and was speaking crossly to him. Clio could not hear Teddy's attemped answer or Helen's objections. Then she saw Helen send the child homeward with an impatient shove.

From the shelter of Teddy's tree, Clio saw Halloran come out the terrace door with Lady Cora on his arm. Helen spoke shortly to them and pounded up the steps to enter the dower house from which they had come.

Hoping not to be seen, Clio put the tree trunk between herself and the couple who were ambling down the lawn, obviously intent upon each other. When they drifted toward the overlook path, she realized she was cut off from any rendezvous with Mr. Stamford. She went hesitantly toward the house, hoping that Helen had joined Eleanor in some room so she would be able to slip upstairs.

Inside, the footman was frozen to deaf stone in his seat at the rear of the hall while Helen complained to Eleanor by the top of the stairs. When she caught sight of Clio below, she exclaimed, *"Really,* Miss Caldicott, you frighten me!"

Clio's mouth rounded in surprise at that word, as she ascended reluctantly.

"Daring to tell my husband that he ought to sell his daubs and filling Teddy with gibberish about elves and such! What will it be next?"

"Oh, Mrs. Linville," Clio cried, trying not to smile at the ridiculous charge. "Mr. Linville's paintings mean so much to him. I think they are wonderful and ought there not to be other people to feel the same way? All I did was suggest he obtain the opinion of someone who should really know."

Coming off the boil, Helen said, "Well, perhaps . . . but all this nonsense with Teddy—elves!— he has to learn to live in a real world, not an imaginary one!"

Clio said earnestly, "Teddy is a darling. I was only trying to give him pleasure. Believe me, if anyone has to live in a real world, it's Clio Caldicott." She thought to herself, *I won't be here much longer.* "Mrs. Linville, that little boy is hungry for your attention."

"Well, aren't you one to tell other people how to live!" said Helen indignantly.

"She is right," said Eleanor unexpectedly. "You neglect Teddy shamefully. Mama thought so, too."

"Neglect!"

"Oh, I do not mean his physical needs. *Maybelle* tends to those. But he is not a little machine. I certainly do not fail Mark like that! In fact, from now on I am going to pay more attention to him."

"Oh, Mrs. Hampden," cried Clio, "you shouldn't—" She broke off, turning scarlet.

Helen smiled maliciously. "Shouldn't what?"

Clio was silent.

Eleanor calmly asked, "What, my dear?"

"I mean—well—Mark has life so easy already—doing whatever he wants—riding like a race jockey—keeping odd hours. I'm sorry. It is none of my business."

"No. No, it is not. I will have to think about this," said Eleanor. "Mama sometimes said—"

At this point Roland catapulted in the front door and shouted from downstairs, "Miss Caldicott! Where are you? Come down at once!"

Although she was not anxious to go to him, she escaped the ladies gratefully.

"Come here," commanded Roland. "Look!"

Clio obediently peeped through a sidelight of the door.

"The dealer is leaving." Words tumbled from Roland. "I think he liked my pictures. He didn't say much, but he took one that he thought a particular collector would buy. If it sells, he wants to arrange an exhibit. Thank you, Miss Caldicott, thank you!"

Overhearing all, Helen flew down the steps and flung her arms around her husband. "Oh, Roland! Which one? Never mind, I would not know, would I?" Her mind obviously dazzled by visions of fame, she added, "I am so glad for you!"

"Is it all right?" he asked, holding onto her.

"Of course it is all right. I just didn't realize . . ."

Over her head Roland smiled at Clio. "It is all due to Miss Caldicott. She told me about Mr. Rawl who was a friend of her father. I wrote—he came."

It being against Helen's nature to apologize to Clio, she said only, "I am so proud of you, Roland." Which was what he surely wanted most to hear.

Thirteen

It was almost eleven when Halloran and Lady Cora reappeared at the dower house, too late for Clio to meet Mr. Stamford since it was close to time for nuncheon. Neither of the elusive pair showed any sign of tender sentiment. In fact, so politely chill were they to each other that one might think there had been a quarrel. They were soon caught up in Roland's good news, however, and any coolness, if there was coolness, was overshadowed by genuine gladness for Roland's good fortune. For none of the scoffers in the household had any doubt *now* that Roland's picture would sell and that he was on his way to fortune. What a change of family attitude!

Eleanor ordered Hood to serve the midday meal on the west terrace. Helen sent word to Maybelle that Teddy must lunch with the family, which was, in a sense, her way of making amends to Clio. It was the best Clio could expect of her.

When Clio went upstairs to her room to freshen herself for the spontaneous alfresco celebration, she found a folded paper mysteriously tucked under her hairbrush where she could not miss it. It said: "Four o'clock. H."

Her pulse leaped. Who would presume to send her secret notes? H? Hugh or Hal? She had never seen the handwriting of either. Since no meeting spot had been indicated, it looked very much as if Mr. Stamford were the author. But why four?

The biggest question was: Should she meet this "H?"

By the time Hood rang his gong, and the seven filed out to the terrace, there was still shade where the bulk of the house blocked the sun from reaching a portion. A colorful buffet, like a glorified breakfast spread, had been placed upon a long table. Chairs and small tables were drawn nearby. Clio had read in ladies' magazines about such meals, but had never enjoyed the delight of this casual elegance.

They were to serve themselves and had begun to take plates when Edward Hampden could be glimpsed riding into the stable yard. An excited chorus hailed him. Handing over his mount to Lady Linville's groom, he strode across the vegetable garden and lawn to join his family and hear the exciting news with which they deafened his ears.

Edward's response was all that was gratifying to his brother-in-law. "I do not know when anything has delighted me more. Our Lady Mary always valued Roland's work."

These last words brought a hush to the group, as the truth of them was known to all the family. They began to fill their plates, Roland taking more than he ever did and then hardly touching it.

Clio was surprised to have Lady Cora choose to sit beside her on a bench for two. The rest distributed themselves hit-or-miss, Hal settling where he could watch two fair ladies, one blond, the other a dazzling redhead. Conversation was vague and sparse.

It being Edward's nature and strength to remain calm, he ate steadily and drank freely of the lemonade that Cook had magically produced. When he had taken the edge from his appetite, he said tranquilly that Lady Linville's man of law would be coming at two o'clock to read the will. There was an immediate hush, into which Edward dropped like a stone, "I have asked Hugh Stamford to be here."

"Why him?" demanded Helen, voicing what the others wondered.

Clio was as surprised as anyone. This official capacity of Hugh's seemed to be driving a wedge between the old friends, Linvilles and Stamfords—a situation to be regretted.

"Because the general asked me to do so," Edward explained. "I, myself, shall be glad to have him here. Perhaps the will may shed some light on our—er—difficulty."

Lady Cora said suddenly, "Halloran and I saw Mr. Stamford this morning at the overlook."

"What was he doing? Snooping?" asked Helen sharply.

Lady Cora spread her hands indecisively, and Hal drawled, "He was doing nothing. Sitting on the wall, smoking his pipe. Said he was 'thinking.' "

"We need more than thinking, but that is a good place to begin," Edward pointed out.

"Oh, when will it all end?" moaned Eleanor.

"End what?" asked Teddy, who had his plate on the flags behind Clio and who had been forgotten.

Helen frowned, but held her tongue.

What was it that made everyone at odds, cross, anxious, unsure? A death . . . or guilty conscience?

"Business, son," said Roland. "It wouldn't interest you."

"Loans?" said Teddy sapiently.

Roland smiled and replied, "Penalties," a hint which Teddy understood perfectly. He asked no more.

When they had nearly finished eating, Mark arrived from the stable to heap a plate and for a change Eleanor did not assist him. He had nothing to contribute to the general conversation. In fact, he was generally ignored, making Clio wonder if family disgust of him made his disposition only worse. He was certainly as welcome as an extra thumb.

"Let us all go view Roland's paintings with new eyes," suggested Lady Cora.

There was a murmur of agreement and they rose to trail languidly toward Roland's loft, leaving Mark to continue his meal. Halloran essayed to approach Clio, but Edward caught her first and drew her aside. "I will appreciate it very much, Miss Caldicott," he whispered, "if you will be present for the meeting with Mr. Foster. Sometimes a disinterested witness is more alert than family."

"But I know nothing!" she protested.

"That is just it. An unbiased outsider may detect nuances that I might miss. Perhaps separate truth from—er—error."

As she hesitated, very reluctant, he added, "You have been helpful to Roland—for which we all will thank you—and I am hoping you will do this for me."

He had said the magic word *helpful* which Clio was unable to resist.

"If the others do not mind, I will be glad to—"

She broke off as the footman led Hugh Stamford from the house. "Mr. Stamford to see you, sir," he said to Edward.

"Hugh! You are early—but always welcome." Mr. Hampden released Clio's elbow and stretched out his hand to shake Hugh's.

Hugh replied, "Thank you, sir. I am early on purpose as there are some points I wish to clear up before Foster arrives." He was natty today in a Devonshire brown morning coat. He carried a top hat. "Lucky to catch you. . . . Good day, Miss Caldicott. Don't go, Mark. My questions are for you."

Surprised, both Mr. Hampden and Clio turned to stare at Mark, who had half risen, although his plate was still laden. He started to sit, then straightened and pushed aside his dish. He wet his lip.

"M—me?"

"You were absent from dinner the night your grandmother fell?"

Mark looked to his father, who nodded.

"Yes, sir. I was a—asleep."

"In his room," Clio offered. "Molly told me."

"When did you go to your room, Mark?"

"I dunno," the boy mumbled.

"Mr. Hampden?"

"None of us saw him," admitted the father. "Look here, Hugh. I did not tell you before as there seemed no connection, but perhaps it will mean something to you. Lady Mary asked me recently if I could raise some money for her."

If he wanted to distract him from his son, he succeeded admirably. Mr. Stamford wheeled to him. "How much money?"

"Four thousand."

"Four thousand what?"

"Er—pounds."

Clio could see Mr. Stamford's jaw tighten.

"You should have told me. This may be important. When was this?"

"The Sunday before she died."

"What was the purpose? Did you raise it?"

Mr. Hampden answered evenly, "I do not know what it was for. She simply asked if it could be done without sacrificing good securities. I told her it could, and that was the end of it."

Hugh Stamford thought a minute, then asked, "Did you tell anyone?"

"No. Private business. After all, she only *asked.*"

The younger man was frowning, pinching his lower lip. "Do you know how Lady Linville's estate is divided?"

"I always supposed in thirds. I never saw her will."
He drew out his watch. "Foster should be here in fifteen minutes or so to read it to us. . . . You may leave
your plate, Mark, but see that you are in the library at
two sharp. You might take a quick wash before meeting
Mr. Foster. Come at the same time, my dear Miss Caldicott. Shall we go indoors, Hugh?"

Mr. Foster had said firmly that he would drive out
from London on Thursday afternoon. Possibly, he
thought bereaved family members needed a few days
to recover from shock and sorrow. At any rate, he had
named two the hour and could be depended upon to
be there on the dot himself. Since he had been en-
trusted with all legal work in the establishment of the
Royal Bank as well as the late Sir Linville's will, Mr.
Foster knew more about the Linvilles than they knew
themselves. He had observed Eleanor, Roland, and
Halloran from birth, two to marry, and he had attended four christenings of Linville grandchildren.
He held his own fixed opinions of each family mem-
ber. His hair was white and his brain still as clever as
it was thirty-five years ago, when Eleanor was born.

When Mr. Foster arrived, Lady Cora received a sa-
lute on her cheek.

Clio, who curtsied repectfully when presented, felt
his keen eyes size her up. She retreated to the window
seat as once before and quietly settled to watch what
transpired. Her position was excellent for viewing everyone, they being seated in a sort of three-quarter
circle before her. Mr. Foster, it was true, was turned
partly from her as he surveyed the circle, but that was
not important, for Mr. Hampden had asked her to
observe family members only.

"Ahem," began Mr. Foster. "I think we might have
the door closed. . . . Thank you, Edward. Now as you
know from the last time we assembled on a similar
unhappy occasion, wills have a language of their

own—some quite obsolete, I fear—but generally accepted. I am going to suggest that in the interest of time you permit me to summarize. Of course the document is open to your scrutiny at any moment. Are you agreed?"

There was a vague murmur of voices and a recrossing of various gentlemen's legs.

"So," said Mr. Foster. He considered the topmost paper of a number in his lap. "Lady Linville establishes annuities for Mr. Hood, Mrs. Plumb, and the longtime cook. It is my understanding that this cook may not have reached retirement age. If she wishes to continue working for a period, Lady Linville directs that her wishes be honored and her annuity held until such time as she does wish to cease her duties.

"Her ladyship wishes no employee of hers to be discharged and asks the present Sir Malcolm to find occupation for any that require it."

"We love our servants," Eleanor said unexpectedly.

Clio could understand this, for she had adored the kind woman who raised her, but she was surprised to find such sentiment in Eleanor.

Mr. Foster said, "Yes. Well." He shifted to the next page. "Now the bank. After Sir Linville's death, ownership of the bank, as well as the presidency, passed to Lady Mary by his will. This was a very unusual circumstance." His tone was disapproving. "Yet I am obliged to admit that his trust in his wife was not an error."

"Indeed not!" exclaimed Mr. Hampden. "Very astute woman."

"Ah, yes. The bank has thrived under her and you, sir. And now, Lady Mary's will was written only a year and a half ago. It is rather a remarkable document. You know Lady Mary was an exceptionally fine woman. She wanted the best for—well, her decision is this."

All eyes were intent upon him. "Her ladyship divides the stock in four equal parts, a quarter each to Roland, Halloran, Eleanor and Edward."

Mr. Hampden cried, "Me!" in astonishment. "How generous of her."

"But that isn't equal!" protested Helen. "It gives Eleanor more."

Clio's glance went from one to another. Roland looked mortified by his wife's outburst. Lady Cora looked contemptuous of her. The other faces showed shock, though whether caused by the will or by Helen she could not be sure.

Mr. Foster said acidly, "Perhaps I had better read her exact words after all. Let me see. Here it is. She felt Edward's 'loyalty, competence, and industry deserve a reward.' "

The family was silent. Eleanor reached out to squeeze her husband's hand.

"Let me add personally, as one who follows every procedure of the banking house," said Mr. Foster, "that without Edward there would be no bank."

The silence that greeted this was palpable.

"It is true," croaked Roland.

"And there is the second bank in Wendel," added Hal.

Mr. Foster nodded and told them that division of the stock would apply to both. The persons sitting before him knew so little of the business world that such things as "stock" and "shares" had little meaning. "I must remind you," he said, "that a county banking house does not match a woolen mill for creating wealth. You cannot"—he sent Helen a punishing glance—"expect to expand your style of living. Sir Malcolm received his father's title and estate, as was customary. This is your parents' way of providing cleverly for you."

Clio did not think they looked grateful—at least,

not yet. Subdued they were. She wondered if the modest income each would have would be enough to satisfy Lady Cora. Did she intend to support Hal in a grander manner? Would he pay for marriage by forgoing his aspirations?

Mr. Stamford made no comments. He was seated in another window seat, so that Clio had no view of him except when he leaned forward occasionally, and then it was his profile she glimpsed. She hoped her own face was as devoid of expression as his—no smile, no clenched jaw, no compressed lips. She did not think the family noticed him any more than they did her.

Mr. Foster had other jolts for them.

"There is a qualification on Eleanor's share," he said. "Eleanor is to take title to her quarter *if* she agrees to work regularly and faithfully in the bank for a minimum of two years."

"Two years! As a *clerk?*" she gasped. "For heaven's sake!"

Her husband leaned toward her earnestly. "Don't you see, my dear? Lady Mary wants you to understand banking. Why, if you grasp it the way she did, you could be an immense help to me—knowing people, meeting others, explaining things so women could comprehend. It is really a mistake for men to leave their wives so completely in the dark about the essentials of family finance."

Whatever Mr. Foster thought of this unorthodox theory, he only said, "Precisely. I hope you, Roland, and you, Halloran, will respect Edward's business decisions. One cannot have bickering in a sound banking establishment. I tried to persuade Lady Mary to avoid deadlocks by an uneven stock distribution, but she would have it this way. Besides, she said that Edward has shown what he can do."

"My mother understood us better than you, sir,"

Roland assured him. "We never question Edward's judgment."

Mr. Hampden flashed Roland a grateful look which was answered by an affectionate smile.

"That so?" murmured Mr. Foster. "Well. So much for the bank. Lady Linville's personal funds are not great and she has disposed of them in an unusual way. Now Mark . . . if Mark applies himself to his books and gains admission to Cambridge or Oxford, he is to receive a curricle and pair. For every pound he earns outside his home between now and his completion of a degree, he is to receive an additional pound, up to a total of one thousand. Any money for which he does not qualify shall revert to Theodore—er, Teddy."

Mark's mouth had fallen open.

"You must prove yourself, young chap," the solicitor said, eyeing him severely. "Lady Linville also leaves one thousand to Helen, on the condition that she give up all offices in all organizations until Teddy matriculates at Eton. This is another trust arrangement. Helen gets the interest, but not the principal until the condition is fulfilled."

By now everyone, including Clio and Mr. Stamford, was speechless at her ladyship's control from the grave. Helen, who had nothing of *her own*, showed a face of elation blended with chagrin. She looked as though she might rocket to the moon if anyone so much as touched her.

All Mr. Foster had to tell them seemed long and involved to Clio. The actual will must be excessively wordy if what he had spoken was in the interest of saving time. And there was more to come.

"The remaining assets of Lady Linville's estate are divided three ways between Eleanor, Roland, and Halloran, as you would expect. There is just one more thing to tell you—about Roland's third. He is to receive two thousand—one a year for two years—*pro-*

vided he devotes those two years to the study of art and attempts to put his talents on a paying basis. At the end of two years he receives the balance of his share. Lady Linville felt sure Roland would accept this challenge. If he does not, the entire amount is to be held in trust for Teddy, with Roland allowed the income for his lifetime."

They could not believe he had finished. There was a frozen stillness about them. Finally Edward spoke, "I am the only one she did not chastise," he said unhappily.

"Don't be blue about it," Helen mumbled.

Eleanor said she and Edward had got most.

"It's all right," Hal answered, his color high. He had been neither chastised nor praised. "Edward is one of us. There is enough for all. Not riches, but enough. What a beautiful, thoughtful will!"

Mr. Hampden observed, "One and one and two make four."

"You are right!" exclaimed Mr. Stamford, springing to his feet. He and Edward exchanged comprehensive looks.

Uncertain, Eleanor asked, "What do you mean?"

"One thousand pounds for Mark, one thousand for Helen, two for Roland," said Edward Hampden. "This explains why she wanted to raise four thousand. She was worried about her family and wanted to do something for them."

Eleanor's face lit up. "And Miss Caldicott to keep her company so we need not be anxious about leaving her alone! How wonderful and caring she was! Oh, God!" She sobbed once and flooded with tears.

While Edward sought to comfort his wife, the others circulated erratically and conferred among themselves. Mr. Stamford approached the solicitor, and while he pitched his voice quite low, Clio being near heard him say, "Not a likely motive among them."

Mr. Foster was more cautious in his assessments. "So it would seem. Tell your father to keep in touch with me."

"Yes, sir," replied Mr. Stamford. He turned to Clio with a small bow, a slight tilting from the waist. "Nice to have seen you again, Miss Caldicott. Will you excuse me? It is three-thirty and I have an appointment at four."

Fortunately, she was not obliged to answer, for her poise was slipping. The gentleman had gone rapidly from the library and from the house. Through the window under which she had sat she saw him swing onto a sleek black horse and trot down the driveway without a backward glance.

Before Clio turned from the window, Halloran came up behind her and asked what she was looking for outside.

"It was Mr. Stamford. I saw him ride off."

"Eh? Gone already? Wonder why the devil Edward felt obliged to ask him here this afternoon."

Clio looked up into Hal's handsome face with its troubled eyes. "Isn't he your friend?"

Hal shrugged impatiently. "Oh, of course, forever and a day, but it is humiliating to have a friend hear shortcomings of one's family."

"He heard none about you," she reminded.

"Nor anything good either!" He twisted his neck as if tension had put a crick in it and grumbled, "Humiliating to have the family poverty laid bare."

Irate, she cried, "Don't speak to me about poverty. I am more familiar with stretching shillings than you are!"

He seemed honestly surprised. "It does not sound paltry to you?"

"Paltry! I doubt my father had one quarter as much, yet he managed to live as a gentleman. We had sufficient to eat, sir!"

Halloran began to laugh. "All right, all right. Do not get all fluffed up like an angry cat. With the right help I shall manage tolerably." His eyes turned toward Lady Cora and Clio wondered if she were the "help" he meant.

Eleanor came up to them then, her face the happiest Clio had seen it. "Have we shocked you, my dear?"

"No, indeed. The will seemed most well designed."

"I should have known it would be," Eleanor admitted.

"Yes," agreed Clio. "I was particularly struck by Lady Linville's tender care for her servants. It was good to hear her plans. They have been troubled and uncertain if you would want them to stay here."

Eleanor was surprised by this new thought. "Of course we want them! Where are my wits? Thank you, my dear girl, for reminding me. How do you know this?"

"Little things were said. They would never complain to you, though they seem worried about the future. Molly dreams of becoming an abigail, I think."

Her expression rueful, Eleanor said, "I have been too wrapped up in my own grief to consider the servants as I should. I will go and set their minds at rest this very minute."

Roland and Helen were in deep conversation, seated at the far end of the room. In a corner Mr. Hampden was offering Mr. Foster and Lady Cora a glass of wine. When Mark spoke at Hal's elbow, Clio seized the chance to ease away. She heard Mark say, "Uncle Hal, should I have a tutor?" Lady Linville's designs were taking effect already.

How long would it take Mr. Stamford to reach the overlook, if that were his destination?

Hoping not to be noticed, Clio slipped out the front door and hurried along the carriage drive to the stables. From there she followed the woodland path to the overlook.

Mr. Stamford was not there.

Fourteen

Peeking cautiously over the wall, Clio scanned the road below. The part of it she could see bore no traffic. Was she silly to expect Mr. Stamford? Suppose Halloran should come. Would he be surprised to find her here when they could easily have talked in the house? If *he* had been the one to leave the note for her, was she a fool to come to a clandestine meeting?

She sat upon the wall, intending to wait a few minutes. *I wish,* she thought, *there were someone to advise me.* It was frightening to be a female alone in the world. After her papa had died, the housekeeper, who had virtually raised her but for whom there were no longer funds, went to live with a sister in Kent. Thank heaven for Mr. Lambton who had brought her together with Mrs. Mellow! Now, by her own daring, she was entangled here and General Stamford wished her to stay until the circumstances of Lady Linville's death were explained. It did not look as if any of the family were involved in anything so alarming as *murder,* yet the death was still unexplained. Would they ever know what happened?

The cracking of a twig made her look toward the woodland path as Mr. Stamford came from it. "So it was your note!" she exclaimed.

"Whom did you expect?" he demanded, taking a seat beside her. "Halloran?"

Flushing, she said it might have been a game of Teddy's.

"Calling himself 'H' and sending a note to your room? I doubt he would think of all that, even if he can write and punctuate 'four o'clock' correctly."

"All right! I should have known *you* are capable of writing the words, but whether you were *correct* to call me to a secret meeting remains doubtful."

"I have never," he responded solemnly, "hurled a pretty young lady from a cliff."

It was not a threat to her life that she feared, but to her reputation.

"I thought," she said with dignity, "that we might have information to exchange."

"Do we? I certainly have some for you. But you go first."

"Where shall I begin? Well, to exonerate myself, Lady Linville's address book has Mrs. Mellow's name in her ladyship's handwriting. Any of the family can tell you that."

"Yes. I saw the book. Go on."

Clio said she had been thinking hard. "If you would just write Mrs. Mellow for confirmation! I can give you her address." She frowned in concentration. "Only this afternoon Mrs. Hampden suggested that Lady Linville might want me with her to free *them* for what she had planned for them to be doing."

"Possibly," allowed Mr. Stamford. "I am really not convinced she needed companionship. She lived alone a while in that huge Hall after Sir Linville died. There has always been Mrs. Plumb, of course, but as devoted as she may be, she could not be intellectual companionship."

"Someone to share meals with?" suggested Clio. "That can be a lonely time."

He shook his head. "The family would not miss

meals. I wonder if she could have been afraid and wanted you to protect her."

"And how much protection would I be? Ridiculous!" said Clio impatiently.

"You could have tried batting those pretty gray eyes at any assailant to distract him."

Indignant at such obvious nonsense in a serious matter, Clio quite ignored his attention to the color of her eyes.

"Honestly, now, tell me how I could have defended her from attack?"

He said slowly, "Depends. No one would have pushed her off the cliff if you had been there."

Clio shivered. "Do you really think someone did that?"

"I do not know," he said. "What motive could there be? There is not enough money in Lady Linville's estate to generate greed. Unless . . . someone had a need . . . debts. Gambling debts, for example. Halloran flies pretty high. Could he—"

"No!" she exclaimed, shocked.

"My girl, you do not understand the ways of young bucks."

"No, and I don't want to. Pray remember that Hal is trying to raise money for an expedition to the Near East. He would not waste tuppence on gambling."

Mr. Stamford admitted the likelihood of that observation. "We cannot even talk about a 'vagrant in the neighborhood' since the overlook is too high above the lane to attract a stranger. I wonder about the servants."

"You mean, suppose Lady Linville caught one thieving or something?" she asked.

"That is what I meant," he said, "but it is hardly worth consideration. You did not know her. She would sooner set the guilty one *straight* than call the constable." He chuckled. "I myself would sooner face the constable than answer to her ladyship!"

"A temper?"

"No, an overpowering force. There isn't even any pilfering or poaching in the neighborhood. If a man was sick, or injured, or down on his luck, Lady Linville would see that his family had what they needed."

"Oh," cried Clio, "how could anyone kill such a person?"

"It seems impossible, yet she died before her time. Father and I intend to learn why—and how. You may think me bloodthirsty, if you choose." He sprang up and began to pace restlessly about the small pebbly oval of the overlook.

What Clio thought was that Mr. Stamford was a young man who never abandoned the pursuit of truth, while she wrestled with her own inclination for a quick peace.

"Mark was not at dinner the night Lady Linville died," she volunteered regretfully, "because he was lying drunk on his bed."

He slid to his former seat beside her. "How do you know that?"

"Molly told me. I did not like to be specific before his father this afternoon. Molly went into his room to light a lamp for the evening. She did not see him, you understand, but the alcoholic fumes told the tale and she ran out. She knew what the odor meant. She had this experience with him before, I think."

Mr. Stamford bobbed his head in a series of quick jerks. "Yes, I suspected as much. There is a tavern at the south end of town—very popular with the locals. I inquired there, but the barman said he had not seen Mark, and he had no reason to lie. Let me think."

As she waited, Clio imagined the gears meshing in his head. She realized that the general would never have deputized his son unless he had confidence in his reasoning.

"When did Mark return to the dower house?"

"No one seems to know," she said.

"It may be," he said, thinking as he spoke, "that the reason Lady Linville went to the overlook was to watch for him. Father says that no one from our home saw her, incidently. Now, if she was watching for Mark or for your coach which was late, she would be facing south. She would not have seen Mark, or he her, because I have an idea that Mark had visited a rum sort of drinking den to the north where he was less well known. A low place—no questions asked. His route home would not take him past the lookout."

Clio asked, "Is there any hope for Mark?"

"That is difficult for me to say. His surliness annoys me so much that I have a problem in hoping—wishing—anything good for him. There! Does that shock you, kind lady?"

"No, because I have to admit the same feeling. But I so slightly know Mark that I must lean on Lady Linville's view of him. If she thought him redeemable—and she should know better than I—then there must be some virtue in him. What bothers me is that she was not more outspoken to Eleanor."

Mr. Stamford said, "Perhaps she was. Eleanor has been kind to you I think? I've known her forever. Generally very dispassionate and pleasant, but with the stubbornness of a donkey. She has a blind spot about Mark."

They sat in companionable silence until Mr. Stamford spoke his thought aloud. "I wonder if Mark was riding his horse that day or driving."

"Does that matter?" asked Clio, surprised at the direction of his interest.

"It could. Let us not forget that Lady Linville had written that she would have someone meet you at the inn. If she sent her groom—well, servants gossip. You were to be an accomplished surprise for her family. She may have chosen Mark, who seldom speaks to anyone, and in that case he would have had her tilbury or the dogcart. The groom will know. I'll see what he has to say."

"You mean he was charged with fetching me and *forgot?*"

"Possibly." He grinned suddenly. "He had not seen you yet." She did not miss this flattering hint.

To change the drift of the conversation she asked, "How did you reach this overlook without being seen?"

"This afternoon when I left the dower house I rode down the driveway to the lane and turned toward Scudderfield. I grew up in the area, you must remember, and know it well. South of the cliff is a ravine which separates it from the lower hills near town. I rode my horse halfway up the ravine, tethered him there, and climbed a steep path to meet you here."

"Oh, yes," she replied, "I recall passing a branch path when I first found the overlook. Must you be *furtive,* sir?"

He gave her a reproachful look.

"To pry into old friends' affairs is embarrassing to me and annoying to them. I think the less they see of me, the better. If you were watching the road for me, I must already have passed."

Since Clio could not admit to watching for him, she said hastily, "What about the servants? Can we truly eliminate them?"

"It seems we must. At the cottage there is Maybelle, who is always busy with one or all of Roland's three children—and a houseboy presently at home with a cough caught from the children—and a cook—"

"Cook! Why are Roland and Helen always dining at the dower house?" she interrupted.

"I daresay Helen prefers the higher style. Her own cook is a poor creature, afraid of her shadow, and prone to hiccoughs if asked to explain anything. I believe we may dismiss her as a candidate for crime. Now, you asked about Halloran's valet. He has one, of course, but has given him leave to visit his family in London while he himself rusticates in the country. Mr. Hampden makes do with the services of Fralke—fashion means nothing to him. Mark would prefer a curricle to a valet, though he has neither at this point."

"What about gardeners?"

"One who comes down from the hall as needed—so gentle that he hates to pull up weeds. Count him out."

"And the men in the stable?"

"What a question-box you are! Two boys, neither one large enough to overpower Lady Linville. Her groom followed her here from her childhood home. Likely to attack her? I think not."

Clio sighed. "So we have a crime without a criminal."

"Maybe not."

"But that leaves us with an accident, which seems unlikely when the wall is so broad and she knew it so well. Will you keep searching for ways and reasons?"

Mr. Stamford said he had promised himself to do so. "There are still some questions to be answered."

"Yes!" exclaimed Clio. "And I forgot to tell you some other things I have discovered. You distracted me with your talk of servants. It is more about Mark. You see, I have noticed that Mark is in the habit of disappearing except for meals. When he went out last night it occurred to me that he must have some way of getting back inside after Hood has locked the house. So this morning I examined his windows from outdoors."

"And?"

"There is no way to reach them from the ground."

He said, "Yes, I saw that, too."

Deflated, Clio said, "I might have known you would. And I hoped to be so helpful." In response to an intense look from Mr. Stamford, she continued in a small voice, "What don't you know?"

"The exact time Lady Linville died," he replied immediately.

"She was alive at six-thirty, according to Mrs. Plumb," Clio told him. "Fralke brought up her tray and Mrs. Plumb stayed to see her start to eat, then she went down for her own supper. The family—except Mark—was at the table by then. No one saw her leave the house, I believe."

Mr. Stamford said, "Ah! Thank you. Things begin to fit, though we still do not know when Mark returned and when her ladyship died. When I get some answers about Mark's departure from the den up the river, times will narrow down. Did Molly say what time she found him in his room?"

"No. I suppose she may have a regular hour for lighting lamps. Some time between eight-fifteen and eight-thirty Mr. Brill and I drove past the cliff. There were lanterns burning but nobody was around. How was Lady Linville found?"

"A tinker, coming from the next village up the river, found her, stopped to verify her death, and came straight to the constable like a good citizen. He did not carry a watch. He says it was just after seven, at a guess. Drove his wagon back with the constable's horse tied behind. They set the lights and while the tinker took the body into town, Constable Tully rode to notify the family. You might almost have met the Linvilles on their way to town."

Clio shook her head. "We did not meet a soul."

They sat a few moments without speaking. How sad it was, Clio thought, that this beautiful spot, half-circled by lush foliage and open to the whole western

world, should be the scene of tragic death. Would the
Linvilles ever want to idle here again?

That Mr. Stamford was thinking along more practical lines became evident when he said, "Alive at six-
thirty, dead at seven or so. Lady Linville must have
slipped from the house as soon as Plummy left her.
The family was at dinner, the servants generally ac-
counted for. I am afraid we need to know more about
Mark."

Clio shuddered. "A *boy* . . ."

"If not Mark, then suicide," he said. "Either way,
tragic." He sprang to his feet abruptly. "Will you wait
while I question the groom? No, you must not stay
here alone. Come with me." He stretched out his
hand.

Clio's legs were not quite long enough for her feet
to rest flatly on the pebbles at the wall. She sat with
one toe pressing into the pebbles and the other foot
tucked up behind it. Without her realizing, one foot
had gone to sleep. As she rose obediently, she staggered, twisted, struck her knee against the wall, and
pitched outward with a gasp. She had a brief, horrify-
ing view of jagged gray cliff and brown lane far below.
Then miraculously Mr. Stamford seized her and
hauled her back against himself.

"Oh, my God! My God!" he cried. His left arm
about her waist held her tightly to him. His right hand
pressed her head against his chest.

Faint with shock, trembling, she made no effort to
draw away. Time and place had lost all meaning. Eyes
closed, she sagged against him, knowing only that she
had come face to face with death and yet survived.
Impossible. But true, blessedly true.

Through her ear upon his vest she could hear the
thunderous pounding of his heart . . . or was it her
own? No, it must be his for it sounded large . . . and

deep. Her own was fluttering in her throat. And her mind came . . . and went.

As her dizziness subsided, Clio heard him distraughtly whisper, "I thought—I thought—I never thought—you'd never—I *forbid* you to sit—"

Forbid?

She raised her head, forcing him to remove his hand, though he still encircled her body with his arm.

"Never put me through another moment like that again!" he said harshly, and almost as if he surprised himself, bent his head to kiss her softly, tenderly, compellingly, healingly, making her feel wholly safe, wholly alive to a life worth living.

There was only one kiss, for Mr. Stamford heard what she had not, voices approaching from the lawn.

"Quick!" he commanded, hurrying her into the woodland path, almost sweeping her off her feet. Her steps were shaky, but with his arm to steady her she managed to walk toward the stable yard. By unspoken agreement, they made as little noise as possible. No one followed.

At the edge of the woods Mr. Stamford asked if she felt secure enough to continue walking without leaning upon him. "It would not do, I think, to give the impression that we have come from a rendezvous— which of course we have. May I break off a few branches for you since you are collecting them, due to a city dweller's fancy?"

"Perfect," she agreed, feeling no difficulty in walking on clouds. She waited while he gathered assorted branches and gave them to her.

"Do you realize," he murmured, "that your experience may have explained Lady Linville's *accident?*"

She stared at him. "You mean Lady Linville may have sprained an ankle or twisted a knee or leaned too far?"

"Something of that sort, yes. It would be the best

answer for a sad event. No one to blame. No one to feel blame."

She sighed and nodded.

He said briskly, "I will just go along and see what the groom can tell me about Mark. Will you wait a few minutes and then come strolling from your—er—horticultural expedition?"

She said she would do as he asked if he would guarantee to tell her what he discovered. She admired his long, smooth stride as he crossed the stable yard.

Fifteen

Clio watched Mr. Stamford disappear into the entrance of the carriage house. She was beginning to feel calmer and steadier though she could not bear to review in her mind as yet the terrible moment when the cliff face flashed before her eyes. The whole experience, she knew, was something she must keep secret from the Linvilles, for mention of it would bring their own grief crashing back upon them like a tidal wave. Besides, she was reluctant to let them discover her appointment with Mr. Stamford in such a secluded place.

He had been quick and strong and obviously aghast, but she must not make the mistake, she told herself firmly, of reading more into his alarm than concern for an endangered girl.

She saw Mr. Stamford come from the carriage house and cross to the stable, presumably not having found Lady Linville's groom. There he remained so long that she began her own trek across the open space and was just passing the stable door when the two men halted beneath its lintel.

Mr. Stamford said politely, "Good day, Miss Caldicott."

The groom touched his cap.

Having understood Mr. Stamford's message, all was well and not to linger, she smiled and proceeded to the gateway of the vegetable garden. She had intended to dispose of the greens which she carried, and which had served their turn, by leaving them under the hedge that separated the garden from the stable area. Unfortunately, Eleanor and Cook were conferring in the garden. They looked up in surprise to see her bearing down on them with a green bouquet.

"Oh, Mrs. Hampden," she exclaimed quickly, "are these common in this area? They are new to me."

"Common enough," replied Eleanor with noticeable lack of interest. "They won't last long in water, if that is what you had in mind. You must choose from plants and trees in the parkland for a bouquet."

"You can't eat *those*," said Cook who had no respect for anything that was not nourishing.

Eleanor laughed at the humor of Cook's attitude. "We are selecting vegetables for the next few meals. This is something my mother did. I know next to nothing about what is not ripe or what is overripe and must be used yesterday."

Cook said parenthetically, "Always make soup."

"I care so little about vegetables," Eleanor told Clio, who wondered just what Eleanor did care about beside her son. "Suppose you decide, Cook," she continued. "Let us sit and rest on the lawn till lunch time, Miss Caldicott. Can you send us something cool to drink, Cook?"

Cook, patently pleased to be left supreme over the vegetable plot, promised to send orgeat.

Relieved to be done with housekeeping, Eleanor led Clio to the west front, where they dragged chairs to the shady side of the beech. Lady Cora came from the overlook path to join them.

"I never realized," said Eleanor, "how many details Mama had to cope with."

While Lady Cora chatted lazily with her hostess about domestic affairs, Clio speculated about the titled lady. She had obviously come from the overlook, and as two voices had interrupted Mr. Stamford and herself, it was logical to guess Lady Cora had been walking with Halloran. But where was he now? She made a bet with herself that sooner or later he would appear from the stable yard as craftily as she had done. He would not know she had had a spectacular meeting with Mr. Stamford, whereas *she* could indulge in wild guesses about him and Lady Cora. Had he made a formal offer? Cora seemed quite composed, even subdued.

"The dower house is lovely, and all ran so smoothly under Mama's hand," Eleanor was saying, "but somehow I miss the cottage. Edward and I were so happy there. It is small, yet large enough for us. You haven't seen it, have you, Miss Caldicott? I might take you down—"

"Oh, no!" interrupted Clio. "I would not be welcome there!"

Lady Cora chuckled. "That's right. Why stick your head in the tiger's mouth?"

"But Helen doesn't own the cottage," protested Eleanor.

"She thinks she does," Lady Cora answered flatly. "If you like the cottage so much, why not trade places? Malcolm would not care."

Eleanor was astounded. "Trade places! How could we?"

Clio thought it was sheer inspiration. She heard Lady Cora say, "Simple. Helen moves here. You move there. She will *adore* the local distinction. You and Edward will be cosy again. I daresay Malcolm will let Edward build a convenient stable for you. Edward will like the independence. Roland will be closer to his loft."

"You have thought of everything," declared Eleanor. Her cheeks had become pink with excitement.

"Molly—" began Clio.

"Oh, yes, Molly. I have already spoken to her and made her my abigail as you suggested. If she tries to turn me into a fashion plate, I shall have you to blame."

Lady Cora asked, "Fashion plate?"

"Yes, out of the ladies' journals—only the *best* designs, you must understand. Molly is upstairs right now making a study of my wardrobe." Eleanor was laughing.

"Well, begin with your hairstyle," directed Lady Cora frankly. "I love you, my dear Eleanor, but you do not make the most of yourself. I declare, you haven't altered your hair arrangement in seventeen years."

"But what," objected Eleanor, "can a village lass know about style?"

"She can look at pictures. What do girls do more often?"

Yes, thought Clio, *and she can look at you, Lady Cora.* She did not suppose Eleanor Hampden would ever be animated, but there was a very good chance Molly would make her into a perfect picture—enough to make Edward think about something more than pounds and pence.

"We must make a plan to present to Edward. He prefers things to be all spelled out," said Lady Cora decisively. "Miss Caldicott, could you find paper and pencil?"

"Find" was a polite way of saying "fetch." Well, Clio was glad to do it. When she returned from the office, Lady Cora had moved a small table into their spot of shade.

"You are so efficient, Cora," Eleanor observed, neither assisting nor objecting.

"I have learned to be. I am mistress of a manor, remember. With a system, details are easily handled. Let us talk about what servants are needed."

Eleanor said she would rather talk about the pretty cottage. "It has pastel walls—so light and cheerful—and satinwood furniture that Mama gave me from the Hall when I was married."

"Why did you leave your things for Helen?" demanded Cora.

"Mama had already furnished this house and I did not like to seem critical of her taste, which is very pleasing."

Lady Cora said sternly, "I command you to take first choice of both houses. If Helen wants new things let her spend her inheritance!"

"I do not think that is what Mama meant," objected Eleanor.

"It is what I mean," retorted her ladyship.

Clio was wide-eyed.

"Now list the servants as we divide them, Miss Caldicott," directed Lady Cora. "Hood will retire, I'm sure. Eleanor will have Molly for her abigail—that is a capital idea—and what do you say to Fralke for Edward? Edward is used to him and has no more desire than Roland to cut a dash. Wouldn't you say Molly and Fralke can double in other duties, such as serving meals and dusting?"

Eleanor agreed weakly.

"You will be busy at the bank," Lady Cora reminded. "These two should keep things in order. What about Cook? Will she retire?"

Eleanor said Cook was partial to Edward for his uncritical appetite. "I believe she will come to us for a year or two, Cora, but we cannot ask her until Edward approves the whole plan."

"Well, we are preparing a plan now, and Edward shall approve it tonight!"

Never had Clio seen people and complicated matters handled so expeditiously. "A groom?" she suggested.

"Mrs. Hampden will take her mother's."

"Will I?" squeaked Eleanor.

"You will. And there's your staff, Eleanor! Start another page, please, Miss Caldicott."

Helen and Roland would have Maybelle for the children, their present houseboy, and possibly Miller, if Miller was willing. Eleanor protested that was not enough, and Lady Cora, knowing it wasn't, declared Helen could find her own staff. "Let me see the lists, Miss Caldicott. Thank you." She scanned the two sheets. "You and Helen both use the laundry maids from the Hall, do you not? There! It is all arranged. Put on your prettiest frock tonight, Eleanor, and let Molly do whatever she may please with your hair. Edward will never think to say 'no' to you."

The three ladies luxuriated in work well done, washed down with orgeat.

It was into this atmosphere of self-satisfaction that Clio ventured to ask, "What about Mrs. Plumb?"

Eleanor looked stricken with shame, and Lady Cora bleated, "Good God! We forgot Plummy. Now, Eleanor, do not be upset. Our plan is not public knowledge yet. I believe I can guess what Plummy would like."

"Some sort of work?"

"No, of course not. I feel sure she would like her old room at the Hall and a chance to spoil Malcolm's children. He is fond of her, you know, very fond. She spoiled *him* without really spoiling him, not ruining him, you understand. If or when her health fails there will be many servants to take care of her at a large establishment like the Hall."

Truly, Lady Cora was never at a loss. Clio marveled. Would this beautiful, affirmative creature structure Hal's life with equal success?

"Put these pages in your pocket—or your reticule— or your sleeve so you can have them to show Edward.

I have no doubt he will like the scheme. Let me handle Helen."

"I would be grateful if you can," Eleanor confessed.

There was no lunch out of doors today. Mark was absent. Edward did not come home. Halloran came promptly when the gong sounded and chose a seat beside Clio, which made her more uneasy than had dinner with the vicar, for instead of Hal's watching from across the table, she had Lady Cora's contemplative scrutiny to bear.

Eleanor's excitement, only partially concealed, did not draw Hal's attention, as he had problems of his own to resolve. When the ladies had finished eating and were heading for the stairs to hear Molly's condemnation of Eleanor's clothes, he caught Clio's elbow and whispered softly, "May I talk with you?" Reluctantly, she accompanied him to the terrace where they would be visible from any western window and could not be considered improper. The situation of a young female companion, thought Clio, was a difficult middle ground between servant and lady.

As once before, they walked to and fro, and Halloran argued with himself.

"I am in a perfect torment! My mother's will makes it possible for me to meet the costs of new exploration, which you know is my dream. Am I a fool? To be honest with you, I must admit that my funds won't last indefinitely. Shall I go or stay, Miss Caldicott?"

"It is not my place to—" she began stiffly, annoyed to be involved.

"Someone must help! I cannot decide. This is *wrenching.*"

"You choose which coat to wear, which horse to wager upon, whom to make your friends! Of course you can decide. Whose future is it?"

"Mine, I suppose, but not mine alone—Cora—my family—"

She had heard that name "Cora" and it kept her silent. She strongly suspected that in a war of wills Lady Cora would triumph. Whether, in that case, either one would be happy, she did not know.

"Do you think I am unreasonable?" he persisted.

"No," she said, preferring *unreasoning* to unreasonable.

"Did your father believe archaeology to be worthwhile work?"

"Certainly. The officers of the British Museum will tell you that much," she replied. "There are marvels to be discovered, and whether whole or broken—according to my papa—they are a precious part of man's history. It is not for me to say if you are the one destined to find them. Such shilly-shallying! You will never find treasure or your own true self unless you decide *something.*"

He was tall, solidly built, with superb address and lively intelligence. Why should his mother not think him capable of success in any field he might choose? Lady Linville's views of her family, otherwise, were right to the mark.

"In a similar case would you go?" Hal asked.

She frowned. "I might or I might not. What matters is that you, yourself, want badly enough to make a try. Now, don't ask me any more. I haven't been to Oxford or circulated with the Ten Thousand or taken a Grand Tour. My opinion is without value."

"I value it," he insisted.

She stamped her foot. "Oh, decide anything. Don't waste time trying to peel an onion." With that, she wheeled away and ran into the house, leaving Halloran to roam about the clifftop lawn, with jaw tight, eyebrows colliding, and head bent, strong hands clasped behind him.

Lady Cora's plan for Eleanor to dazzle her husband came to nothing. First of all Eleanor refused to relin-

quish her mourning black. Molly did the best she
could with a touch of pink to her mistress's cheeks
and judiciously applied rice powder. The hair, Molly
averred, would necessitate a trip to a coiffeur in Wendel. Meanwhile, she brushed it till it glistened and
coiled it in a soft, loose, becoming knot.

Eleanor looked exceedingly well, but Edward
scarcely noticed as he intended to, and did, call the
five to meet him in the Gold Parlor after dinner.

"You, too, Mark," he said with unusual firmness.

Puzzled and chilled by his manner, they obeyed,
Eleanor clutching her reticule with the wonderful
plan inside it.

"Hugh Stamford," he began severely, "called on
me at the bank today to give me shocking information.
If any of you knew it already, I should have thought
you would have done me the courtesy of sharing it
with me since it concerns me so closely."

He glared at Mark. "I am informed that my son has
been *sneaking* from the house at all hours to patronize
the lowest sort of drinking dens—the tavern in Scudderfield and, more recently, a squalid dive north of
here."

Eleanor gasped, but said nothing.

Halloran wore a faintly amused expression which
slid into chagrin when Edward continued. "We had
thought Mark asleep the night Lady Mary died, but
he was lying drunk upstairs. I can bear the shame only
because he did not leave the foul place until sometime
after her ladyship's accident and so could not have
been concerned in it. Am I correct, Mark?"

Mark, very white, assented in a cracking voice, "Yes-
sir."

"At least you admit it. I have gone myself to verify
this. Hugh suggests that Lady Mary may have gone to
the overlook to watch for you, Mark. What do you have
to say to that?"

Mark was heard to mutter that his grandmother had asked him to meet the young lady who was coming on the five o'clock stage, but he forgot.

"Forgot!" cried Mr. Hampden. "You had the dog-cart for that particular purpose and you forgot! But for this, Lady Mary might not have died. Now, we can only hope it was some sort of accident." To Eleanor, Cora, Clio and Halloran he said, "Mark did not leave the pub until seven-fifteen; she was dead before seven-five."

Tears were streaming down Mark's face.

"Go to your room. I will come up shortly."

The boy lurched to his feet and shambled from the room. They heard him taking the steps by twos.

"I am very much to blame," Edward said bitterly. Eleanor stretched a trembling hand to him and he led her toward the door. "It could have been worse, my dear," he said tenderly, showing no reproach.

When the pair had exited, the three remaining stared blankly at each other. They had nothing to say.

Clio was next to leave. She did not know how long Cora remained with Hal that evening, nor in what mood. She hurried to her room and threw herself upon the bed to think. It was too early for sleep, and in any case her mind was churning vigorously. It seemed that the mystery of Lady Linville's death had been solved. No one believed her to be suicidal, and neither crime nor criminal had been found. But how, she wondered, could one who knew the overlook so well, and who might have been expected to be perfectly careful, have any sort of accident? If a trot was as fast as Lady Linville liked her horse to travel, one would presume she would be careful how and where she walked.

A mouse scratched gently at her door.

"Come in," she said.

It was a Molly mouse. "Oh, miss, I just could not

wait to thank you and there hasn't been a free minute.
Miss Eleanor has promoted me to abigail! And all due
to you, I'm sure."

Clio sat up and smoothed her skirt and pushed back
a lock of hair. "I only dropped a hint," she replied.
"Mrs. Hampden was in a very—er—open mood, what
with Lady Cora filling her with a lot of surprising and
delightful ideas. One more slipped in easily. Are you
happy?"

"As a grig," declared the little maid. "I hope to
persuade her into different gowns, more the thing for
youth and beauty."

Clio laughed. "Just keep dropping those words—
youth and beauty—and your game will be won."

"Well, of course, Miss Eleanor is older than yourself
and we can't expect her to look as though she was
about to make her bow, as Cook says she did eighteen
years ago, but that's no reason to look like a rag-
picker's sack."

"You exaggerate," Clio said. "Do not rush her. She
feels her mother's death deeply and will not want
bright colors soon."

"Yes, miss, I understand. No shocking colors. Mean-
time, we can study styles in *The Lady's Magazine,* which
my sis says Mrs. Stamford takes regular."

"Summer is a good time to persuade Mrs. Hampden
into pastels."

"Pastels, miss?"

"Light colors. Pink, lavender, pale greens and
blues."

Molly said emphatically, "I see. Don't want her to
look like a dowdy. Well, I thank you kindly, miss, for
getting me this chance. Shall I turn down your bed
now?"

Clio waved her away and she bounced from the
room, closing the door with gentle care. Molly had
not heard yet about the proposed move to the cottage,

but Clio did not think she would mind which house she served in, as long as she had command of the wardrobe. It was good to see someone happy in this troubled place!

She moved to a window and looked out upon the serene stretch of lawn with the beech where Lady Cora had made clever plans for Eleanor, and at Teddy's chestnut tree where she had felt carefree for brief moments with him. Had the time finally come for her to leave? She was enchanted with picturesque Scudderfield and the small river and surrounding green hills. London seemed far away. It was the only life she truly knew in depth, yet she could envy the Linvilles their tranquil manor and wonder at their inner turmoil. Had they been at odds with life and each other while Lady Linville was alive? *She,* as comments about her showed, had given enjoyment everywhere, and must—yes, must have known satisfaction herself. Would Lady Linville's plans for her family make *them* satisfied? She thought they would—except for Hal. Her ladyship had forced no plan on him. Was she uncertain? Or could she have been purposely forcing him to make a choice?

Clio's speculations were interrupted by someone tapping lightly at her door. She crossed to it and admitted Lady Cora.

"I am not disturbing you?" Lady Cora asked.

"No indeed. Take the chair and I will perch upon this dressing stool."

"There are things about which I know little," said Lady Cora, seating herself. This surprised Clio, who both admired the earl's daughter and was awed by her. "Tell me," continued Cora, "something about the work of an archaeologist."

Struck anew by the largeness of Cora's character, Clio replied slowly, "Have you not read about Lord Elgin—perhaps met him?"

"No, I have not met him. As to reading about his work, yes, I saw newspaper reports, but I found them tedious. If I sink myself in your opinion, I am going to admit that I took care to read as little as possible because Halloran and I are so at odds about the subject."

Both had to laugh at that.

"I cannot tell you details," Clio said. "Papa talked about the excitement of finding ancient relics after patient digging."

"Did he say how long?"

"To dig, you mean? I never heard exact times. Occasionally it takes years—"

"Years!"

"Yes. Though sometimes a discovery is made by accident. There is jubilation then. Did I not hear that Mr. Linville had been on more than one search? He can tell you more than I can."

Lady Cora said, "Well, you see, I haven't let him talk to *me* because it seemed so childish."

By then, Clio was scandalized. "Oh, no," she protested. "Intense research must come first. The archaeologists must study other finds and ancient manuscripts and maps. Lord Elgin found so much above ground—on the acropolis—waiting to be picked up. He *bought* many great scupltures."

"Then why," asked Lady Cora, "does Hal keep droning on and on about excavation?"

"Because most discoveries are found by digging."

"Sounds demeaning and filthy. Do wives go?"

"Sometimes." Clio answered with a single word, not wanting to discourage nor encourage.

"Where do they live?"

"In nearby villages—which supply workmen—or maybe in huts." She began to giggle. "You should hear Papa's friends, Mr. and Mrs. Hubly, tell about their adventures. They spent a year in a desert with only a tent. Mrs. Hubly would make you chortle with her tales of workmen who could not speak English and strange things to eat. I believe they sometimes burned dung as fuel for cooking."

"Horrors! Did she hate it?"

"No indeed," said Clio. "She dug artifacts right alongside her husband and loved it."

Lady Cora shook her head and said it sounded appalling. "Would *you* enjoy it?"

"I might. It depends," Clio answered. She could not resist adding wickedly, "I would not like scorpions. . . . But generally, it does sound exciting."

Lady Cora regarded her thoughtfully. "Does it demand courage?"

Clio admitted she did not know. "It more likely requires a sense of humor."

Lady Cora stood and gave herself a shake as though ridding herself of scorpions and sand. "I must think about this," she said soberly. "Thank you, Miss Caldicott. Good night."

Was I fair with her? Clio pondered when the door had closed. *Did I present a balanced view of the subject?* She believed Lady Cora was equal to anything to which she might truly aspire.

A note inside her door next morning read:

Good-bye. I have seen him look at you. You would be good for him. Attach him if you can. I have concluded I do not want a husband unless he is surely and wholeheartedly mine.

Sixteen

Clio was still standing in her nightdress, holding the note, when Molly entered with hot chocolate.

"Morning, miss," she said cheerfully. "Just you pop back into bed and have this while I fetch hot water for you. No hurry this morning as Mr. Hampden has moved breakfast up to nine and asked Mr. Roland and Miss Helen to come." When she had seen Clio restored to her bed, she opened the curtains of the room, laid out clothes efficiently, curtsied, and sped away.

It was easiest to obey. Clio sipped her beverage, still shocked by Lady Cora's message. Gone already? If so, Molly did not seem to know, which was odd, because servants usually knew more than their masters. Perhaps Lady Cora had sent a note last night to her groom who was staying with her carriage at the Hall. Had no one heard it call for her in the early hours?

Sunlight streamed into Clio's room. She set aside her cup and drew Cora's note from under the covers. Reading it now, with stronger illumination than had filtered through the curtains, she found not a word changed.

What would everyone think when they found Lady Cora missing? She hoped no one would ever know about the paper in her hands! So baffling! The instructions to *her* were clear. She was to attach Halloran if she could. But the rest was ambiguous. Cora gave no real clue to her own sentiments. Unless Clio herself was very, very careful, three persons could be injured—and others by propinquity grieved.

"I have overstayed my welcome—if I ever had one!" she said to herself. "I must, must leave today. Someone, besides me, will have to explain Lady Cora's disappearance."

When Molly returned with the water pitcher, Clio asked where her trunk had been stored.

"In the cupboard across the hall. But you won't be wanting it, will you, miss? Mr. Hood was saying just this morning that you've been like fresh air in the house."

"It was Lady Linville that wanted me," she reminded. "I ought to go back to London. Is the cupboard locked?"

"No'm. Fralke or I will get the box for you any time you wish, which I hopes won't be soon. Well, it can't be today, seeing as the London coach has already passed through Scudderfield half an hour back."

"Oh!" protested Clio, "so early? When I came from London we were hours late reaching here."

Molly said she must remember that stormy day. "Look at today, miss. Sun bright enough to make one blink. Roads dry, too."

"Is there no other stage?" Clio asked without much hope.

"Just the mail, but that only takes four passengers, and it is always filled before it reaches a little place like Scudderfield."

As they talked, Clio had been dressing rapidly. "Then I must catch the stage tomorrow for sure," she said firmly. "Better have my trunk today so I can start packing."

Molly shook her head regretfully. "If you has to, you has to. Let me button you, miss, and then I'll bring the trunk. You can be sure I won't forget how you helped me!"

Clio's small trunk was no problem for Molly, who soon hefted it across the hall and into the room. "There's no rush, is there, miss? I'll find some time to pack for you. Just you show me what you'll want for traveling," she said. "I must see to Miss Eleanor now." Pride crept into her voice with the words, "see to Miss Eleanor."

Clio smiled to think that Eleanor Hampden would be pressed into a fashionable mold, willy-nilly. She wondered what sort of person young Lady Linville might be. Well turned out, for sure, as a baronet's wife. Why shouldn't a baronet's daughter be just as smart? She agreed with Molly's aims.

Setting aside the brown frock she had travelled in, together with her cloak, she began placing miscellaneous things into the trunk—walking shoes, dancing slippers of black silk, which were never worn, but purchased as a "necessity" by Mrs. Mellow, gloves, ribbons, petticoats, and other underclothes. The rest of her belongings could wait a bit.

It was almost nine. She went through the hall to the main stair, wondering if Lady Cora had been missed.

Not yet.

A place had been set for Lady Cora as usual. Roland and Helen came in promptly to join Eleanor, Mr. Hampden, and Mark, who was looking considerably less slovenly than usual. As they were taking their places at the table, Halloran breezed in to fill his plate from the sideboard.

"Where is Lady Cora?" he asked. "Being lazy?"

When was Lady Cora ever lazy?

Eleanor observed that Cora would not want to miss this meeting. She asked Hood if Lady Cora's abigail was in the kitchen.

"No, madam. I have not seen her this morning."

"Oh? Then, Fralke, will you please knock at Lady Cora's door and tell her she is wanted."

Fralke, who was standing at Eleanor's elbow with a silver dish he was about to pass, said, "Pardon, ma'am. Her ladyship has gone."

"Gone?" said Eleanor blankly.

"Gone!" echoed Hal, swinging around and almost spilling his kippers.

"Her abigail summoned me early to carry down her ladyship's luggage," Fralke reported. "Her carriage came almost at once."

Mr. Hampden asked sharply, "What time was this?"

"Six-thirty, sir," said Fralke, maintaining a disinterested face at a very interesting moment.

"Good God!" exploded Hal. "Who expected this?" His gaze swept the faces at the table, and Clio, with effort, managed to look as baffled as the rest. Lady Cora's note burned in her pocket. Though it should set her on fire, she knew she could not bear to reveal it.

It was astonishing to all that a carriage and four horses could come to the door and not awaken *someone*, though all bedrooms were on the opposite side of the house.

"Plummy may know," said Hal tightly. Thrusting his plate to a corner of the table, he pelted from the room.

"This is so unlike Cora," Eleanor observed. "I wonder if she left a note that I missed. Fralke, will you look in my room—and the office, please."

"What do you know about this, Mark?" his father demanded unreasonably, and Mark, offended to be thought guilty in every case, muttered, "Nothing, sir."

Helen's eyes were sparkling with mischief. "Why, I think Cora is very clever. She has put a fire under Hal, this time!"

Was *that* what Cora had done? Clio's thoughts tumbled over each other as she struggled with motives of people she little knew. Had Cora's departure a purpose that she had not guessed?

Breakfast, as a meal, was a washout. Only Mark continued to eat as they waited for Hal's return, which came soon.

"Plummy knows nothing. I'll take Charger to the Hall, if you don't mind, Mark. Need my riding boots and a faster horse," he said tersely. "May catch her. I had made up my mind to—"

"But which way will you go?" interrupted Edward, trying to inject a little sanity into the situation.

"Toward her manor first," Hal answered. He stuffed a muffin in his mouth and disappeared through the door to the kitchen wing.

One by one, those remaining at the table resumed their meal. No one ate heartily.

"We may as well have our meeting here and now," Edward said, accepting more coffee from Hood. Fralke, who had returned empty-handed from the upper floor, offered cream and sugar. Edward declined both and motioned the servants to leave. When they had vanished behind the service door, he said, "Eleanor and I have a plan which we think you will like." He turned his head toward his son and added, "You need not stay, Mark. We are only going to talk about houses and you won't be interested in those, as I have in mind sending you to London."

"London!" cried Mark, his face glowing as Clio had never seen it do.

"Not for roistering, son, but for intensive study."

Even this seemed pleasing to Mark, one of whose problems was boredom. As his mother was nodding and smiling he assumed what they designed for him was an improvement over Scudderfield. "Yes, sir," he acknowledged promptly and slid from his seat with unusual alacrity.

Edward smiled also—grimly, but at least he did not

frown, which Clio saw as a favorable sign. "Eleanor's and my proposal is to exchange houses with you."

"Exchange houses!" cried Helen, so surprised that the shrill words could be heard through the service door if anyone should happen to be loitering there, as was likely.

Eleanor touched a finger to her lips.

"You can't mean you want the cottage," said Helen, modifying her voice. "Leave this beautiful house? Surely not!"

"But we do," Eleanor answered with a slight smile. "There are only three of us and Mark will be gone most of the time. The cottage was Edward's and my first home together. We were happy in it. I miss the pretty light furniture that Mama gave me."

Helen was chagrined. "Why didn't you say so?"

"I thought you needed it. As to trading houses, I cannot feel right staying here and taking my mother's suite. There are too many memories."

"Would that bother you?" Roland asked his wife.

"No. Truthfully, it would not," she said. "Lady Mary was a very fine person and one does not expect to step literally into her shoes. A *daughter* might feel differently. I can understand that."

With a solemn face Edward added the telling point, "If you move here, Roland will be closer to his loft, and I will be an eighth mile closer to the bank." Which latter observation made them chuckle.

Roland asked sensibly about the cost of maintaining the dower house. "My income will not be what Mama's was."

"I do not see any problem. Malcolm keeps both places in repair for us, and he can afford it. As your paintings sell and the banks increase earnings, we can relieve his load. We can hope Malcolm's wife will have no need of a dower house for a long, long time."

"What about servants—" began Helen, trying to consider all angles.

Edward forestalled her. "What about servants? Eleanor has made lists. Where are your papers, dear?"

Eleanor produced them from a pocket and passed them to Helen, saying, "If my working at the bank takes too much time, I suppose I will have to have a housekeeper, but there are no good quarters for one at the cottage. With your staying home accordingly to Mama's will, you can apply all your managerial talents to housekeeping here."

"She may even enjoy it," said Roland.

Helen did not look sure of any such thing, but she was obviously thrilled at the thought of dwelling in a large and exquisite Georgian house that was known throughout the county.

"Oh, Eleanor," she exclaimed, "let us go down now and tour the cottage with an eye to your comfort, and then we can return here to make plans for us. Have you thought about Plummy?"

"Yes. Cora insists she will want to return to the Hall."

The two ladies, talking congenially for a change, departed by the front door to walk to the cottage. Deep in financial matters, Edward and Roland went off to Roland's loft so that they could have privacy to hammer out details.

Having listened silently to the discussion, Clio decided that the devised switch was very workable. A bit lonesome, she wandered into the office to use the free time for writing a long letter to Mrs. Mellow.

She had not been penning long, when the footman came in. He said, "Beg pardon, miss. Cook wonders if she could have words with you."

Surprised, but willing, she agreed. Apparently Cook was waiting just outside the office door, for she and Fralke exchanged places immediately.

"Oh, miss," said Cook, who had lent the interview a formal air by removing her apron, "Molly says you got her made abigail by saying right words to Miss Eleanor, and I was hoping you could help me."

"Well, if I—"

Clio had no chance or need to finish her sentence, for Cook ploughed on. "I'm not *old* enough for retirement. What would I do with meself? And who would cook for Mr. Edward? Besides, miss, much as I love Mr. Roland's kiddies, to have them underfoot when I was raising a sponge don't bear thinking! Could you speak to Miss Eleanor, miss, and tell her to take me along to the cottage with her?"

So much for "private" family conferences! The proposed moves were known behind scenes, although Eleanor's lists of servant distribution had not been read there.

Clio eased back in her seat, smiling. "Mrs. Hampden said that you and her husband have an affinity—er—kindred feeling about food. She will not part with you, I am sure. Will you be happy with a smaller kitchen and maybe fewer conveniences?"

" 'Deed, yes, miss. Takes half a day to walk acrost *this* kitchen. If I can just take a few of me favorite pots?"

"Mrs. Hampden will want you to do so," Clio promised.

"Thankee, thankee, miss," said Cook fervently. She made a heavy curtsey and departed. Clio heard her say to Fralke in the hall, "No nonsense about Pretty Miss."

Little did Cook guess that "Pretty Miss" was so nonsensical as to go haring off to a strange shire to work for a strange lady, doing she-did-not-know-what duties. Clio shook her head ruefully to find herself returning to a letter which she did not know what it would cost to receive if unfranked. It might never reach Mrs. Mellow, yet it gave her comfort to pour out her troubles to one whom she believed to be her friend.

The letter grew and time passed.

Eleanor and Helen returned from the cottage and began their assessment of the dower house. Helen was so delighted with her prospects of high living that she disputed little that Eleanor might wish to take from the house—a Chinese screen and Dresden china, for example. They gave no thought at all to Clio, who could hear snatches of their conversation as they crossed the entrance hall, back and forth, going from room to room.

The only serious discussion concerned the two portraits of Sir Linville and Lady Mary. After some vague disclaimers on the part of both women, Helen said Roland was very partial to his father's portrait and she felt sure that "he would wish it to stay over the mantel in the drawing room." This was agreeable to Eleanor, who had already envisioned seeing Lady Mary grace the drawing room of the cottage.

They did not take time for the office, as that room, though handsomely furnished, was so utilitarian as to be uninteresting. Chatting about the polish on the steps, the ladies went up to brief Plummy on the latest, wonderful plans, sure that she would approve.

Clio resolved to ask immediately after lunch if someone could transport her to Scudderfield that afternoon to meet the London coach. If Molly was right about the coach schedule, she would have to cast herself upon Mrs. Brill for one night, so as to be there to board early on the morrow.

Shortly before noon Hal returned, dusty and disgruntled. He found Clio in the office by asking Fralke.

Hastily folding her letter and fastening it with a seal as Hal entered, she queried, "Any luck?"

She had read his expression correctly. "None," he said. "I rode top speed on the route to Cora's manor and should have overtaken them—or at least discovered some clue that they were just ahead of me. They were not seen at all—not anywhere I asked. There are a thousand places she could have gone."

"You can search another day," Clio reminded.

"Yes, if I had any inkling . . . Why would she disappear just when I had made up my mind?"

Clio did not reply. She thought she would rather not hear to *what* he had made up his mind, but it seemed he was determined for her to know, for he said peevishly, "I was going to lay down an ultimatum."

Lady Cora would not take happily to ultimata, Clio told herself. However, such—not being common to the lady's experience—might shock her into an uncharacteristic response.

"Do not tell me what it was!" she cried. "If she is not angry with you, she will permit you to find her, and then no ultimatum may be necessary. If she *is* angry, you will have to eat crow or prepare yourself to find someone more amenable. I don't want to hear any more. Go away! Go away!"

He looked offended, and then—to her astonishment—amused. "Good God," he exclaimed. "A little spitfire. Who would have thought those cool gray eyes would ever shoot sparks?"

Grasping her letter to Mrs. Mellow, she erupted from her chair and raced from the office, only to meet Eleanor and Helen at the bottom of the stairs. Simultaneously, Hood's gong rang.

"It is time to eat," Helen said. "You do not want to go upstairs now."

Unable to argue with reason, Clio followed the ladies into the dining salon. In a minute or two, Roland and Mr. Hampden entered the terrace door and met Halloran in the hall. "Did you find her?" the pair asked, to which Hal muttered, "No."

The three joined the ladies at the table. Eleanor and Helen were so excited and buoyed by happiness that they did not detect Hal's strange mixture of gloom and devilment or Clio's tight control. Edward and Roland, both naturally placid, were merely glad to see their spouses' jubilation.

"Where is Mark?" asked Eleanor when she noticed an empty chair.

"Rubbing down the horse I rode so hard," Hal replied. "I promised him a fee and he has earning money on his mind now."

"Oh, excellent," said Edward. "Do not pay him too much, I beg."

Hal swore he was learning to be a perfect miser.

During the nuncheon period a handsome chaise, dusty with travel, and a dark green curricle passed the dower house to halt in Lady Linville's stable yard. The diners at the table had not heard it and so—more or less serenely—addressed their meal.

Mr. Hampden, for all his talk of sharing financial matters with one's wife, said nothing of banking business. He left it to Eleanor and Helen to tell Hal their delight and plans. Hal, for his part, could not be said to have taken much interest. His face was glum. His eyes revealed nothing as he watched Clio sombrously.

As before, he was across the table from her, so to avoid his gaze she kept her attention on her plate, though her appetite was peckish. Only occasionally did she lift her lids for an idle sweep of lawn and western hills.

Fralke had just brought in a fool for their dessert when Clio gasped. All eyes turned her way. "People are on the lawn," she whispered. They were coming from the overlook.

It was an odd way to describe two gentlemen she recognized quite well.

"Why, it's Hugh Stamford," said Mr. Hampden,

"with a gentleman I do not know." He began to rise to his feet. Some air, some style of garb, rendered the older man distinguished. The others rose, too, and Clio with them.

"It's Dr. Dudley!" she cried. "Dear Dr. Dudley!"

Without realizing what she was doing, Clio ran from the dining salon and plunged out the terrace door to hurl herself upon the astonished elder man. There was not a person present, including Hugh Stamford and Dr. Dudley himself, who was not surprised.

"I'm so *glad* to see you! Tell them! Tell them you know me and that I make my home with Mrs. Mellow," she begged.

"Of course I know you, Clio," he responded, holding securely to the distraught beauty. "What in God's name are you doing here?"

All stood gaping around the pair. Dr. Dudley, being an expert physician, read her trembling body for extreme agitation and continued to hold her snugly.

"Lady Linville wrote Mrs. Mellow, asking for me to come to her, and I *did,* only no one expected me and Lady Linville had *died . . .*"

"Ah!" said the doctor. "I am beginning to understand. Let us go inside where we may sit down." As if it were his own house he led the way into the entrance hall, from which Hood wafted them into the drawing room. Dr. Dudley set Clio onto the apricot sofa and though he continued to hold her hand, he allowed Mr. Stamford to present him to Mrs. Hampden and Mrs. Linville and the various gentlemen.

There was a hasty scramble to find seats, while Hood and Fralke unblushingly stationed themselves against the rear wall.

"I think I can explain most of this," Dr. Dudley began. "First, tell me, my dear, if you have Lady Linville's letter?"

"No, sir. It went by accident to York with Mrs. Mellow, who said she had never heard of 'Mary Linville.' "

"Of course she had not," he agreed calmly. "Can you remember what it said?"

"A bit. 'Dear Mrs. Mellow, Henry tells me that you are soon to visit your son, so your—companion, Miss Caldicott—' "

"Henry, eh? Who is this Henry?" he interrupted, smiling.

"Mrs. Mellow did not know."

"Then let me introduce him. Dear girl, I am Henry—though you may always have heard Fran Mellow call me 'Harry.' " He cast a shrewd glance around the circle of perplexed faces.

"Lady Mary and I are very old acquaintances, who did not see each other for many years. She was raising a family here and I was pursuing the practice of medicine in London. Three weeks ago Lady Mary visited her regular physician in Wendel to complain of a minor problem. That is, I say 'minor' because he found no evidence of disease. But she would not be satisfied, so he recommended that she see a specialist in London and gave her several names. Mine she recognized at once, so she chose to visit me."

"But when?" cried Eleanor. "We did not know!"

"The next day."

"Yes, I remember. About three weeks ago she went to London for some concert or other. We did not know she saw a doctor!"

Mr. Hampden cleared his throat and asked the diagnosis.

"She was having some dizzy spells. I found no physical cause for them."

"Medicine—" suggested Hal, hesitantly.

Dr. Dudley looked at the tense faces before him. "None that I could give for a nebulous ailment. I thought, you see, that she was troubled, worried about something. She would admit to nothing like that, but I could not get away from my feeling that *distress* was behind her symptom. I suggested a trip from home— to the Lake District—or a sea voyage. It was at that time I told her about Fran Mellow, widow of my close friend, who was so happy with her young companion, Miss Caldicott."

"Did you tell her I would be alone while Mrs. Mellow was in York?" demanded Clio, who had revived a good deal.

"Yes, I did," he answered.

Roland spoke now in his kind voice. "We had already come to accept Miss Caldicott's story, but I think we owe her an apology as well."

"We do indeed," Halloran agreed, with a serious look in his eyes. The others murmured something similar.

"Perhaps," ventured Dr. Dudley gently, "you know what Lady Linville could not be persuaded to tell me— what troubled her so much that her body reacted with dizziness."

Mr. Stamford looked briefly at Clio. He said, "I have shown Dr. Dudley the overlook. He believes, as I do, that Lady Linville was sitting there and fainted."

Eleanor began to weep. The others looked white and stricken. They could no longer shift the blame to Mark for his youthful irresponsibility. They understood without explanations that their own various failings had directed Lady Linville's actions—her plans—her hopes for them.

Steady as a rock, and least culpable of all, Edward said, "Thank you sir. I'll take my wife upstairs now." He went to her and lifted her to her feet.

"Pray forgive my leaving, Doctor. I must tell Plummy about this," she said and let Edward lead her away.

Everyone began to move about. Mr. Hood hissed at

Fralke, and almost before the last nose had been blown, they had produced the brownest of hot tea.

Clio soon found Mr. Stamford beside her. "Mama said for me to bring you to her," he told her softly.

She nodded thankfully. "I must go away—go home."

"Get your things. I'll bring my curricle round."

Dr. Dudley was holding the others' attention.

She scampered hastily up the stairway and ran along the cross hall to her room to ring the bell. While she waited, needing the footman, she threw the brown dress and other items in the truck and fastened it.

Molly answered the summons. "Oh, miss!"

"We want Fralke for my trunk," Clio said. "Can you get him?"

"Aye," said Molly and ran away without questions.

Before the servants had returned, Clio had taken a few notes from her reticule, wrapped them in a sheet of paper, and pencilled "For my vails" upon it.

Fralke came with a long face and took her trunk away. She followed him along the hall, intending to slip her slim parcel under Eleanor's door, but when she reached that door, it stood open, and she saw Eleanor lying listlessly upon a *chaise longue*. Mr. Hampden was not in sight.

She tapped on the open door. "Thank you for your kindness to me, Mrs. Hampden." Her cloak and bonnet showed her departure was near. "May I leave this money for the servants? Will you see they get it? It is not much, I know, but at least it will show that I have appreciated their—acceptance of an interloper."

"But you must not run off! You have been a real comfort," Eleanor said, rousing herself.

"I have not done anything," Clio mumbled, her coloring becoming pink. "Thank you for making me welcome when I was so unexpected. I have a ride now. Mr. Stamford is taking me to his mother until I can catch a stage to London."

From the landing she peeped down and saw her trunk beside the front door. Mr. Stamford was waiting next to it and Halloran was speaking with him. For a moment she felt a timid desire to turn back and descend another way. Then she took a deep breath and started down. Both men heard her steps and turned toward her.

"Little Miss!" Halloran exclaimed and mounted firmly to meet her a few steps above the bottom. "You are not leaving!"

She nodded.

"Why, Clio, you can't go now," he said, capturing her free hand in both of his with an Old World sort of gesture. It was from the wrist of this hand that her reticule swung between them, with her impassioned letter to Mrs. Mellow inside it.

"I don't belong here," she faltered.

"But you do! There is not one of us that you have not done something for, except . . . perhaps? . . . me, and I am asking you to stay."

Was this some sort of offer? Like none ever made before?

She stared down into his eyes, warm and earnest. The ghost of Lady Cora stood behind him.

Clio looked beyond his shoulder to where Hugh Stamford waited, his face inscrutable.

"I'm sorry, Mr. Linville," she said gently, drawing away her fingers. "I must go."

Mr. Stamford's face became radiant. "I'll put your trunk into my curricle," he said.

"Thank you," she replied primly.

She brushed past Hal, went down the remaining steps, and crossed the hall.

"Good-bye!" she said joyfully to the Linvilles and followed Mr. Hugh Stamford out the door.

More Zebra Regency Romances